M

W9-BUT-523

BOUNTY ON BANNISTER

Center Point
Large Print

Also by D. B. Newton and available from
Center Point Large Print:

The Savage Hills

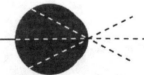

**This Large Print Book carries the
Seal of Approval of N.A.V.H.**

BOUNTY ON BANNISTER

D. B. Newton

CENTER POINT LARGE PRINT
THORNDIKE, MAINE

ISBN: 978-1-64358-102-6 (hardcover)
ISBN: 978-1-64358-106-4 (paperback)

Library of Congress Cataloging-in-Publication Data

Names: Newton, D. B. (Dwight Bennett), 1916- author.
Title: Bounty on bannister / D.B. Newton.
Description: Center Point Large Print edition. | Thorndike, Maine :
    Center Point Large Print, 2019.
Identifiers: LCCN 2018054972| ISBN 9781643581026 (hardcover :
    alk. paper) | ISBN 9781643581064 (paperback : alk. paper)
Subjects: LCSH: Western stories. | Large type books.
Classification: LCC PS3527.E9178 B68 2019 | DDC 813/.52—dc23
LC record available at https://lccn.loc.gov/2018054972

CHAPTER I

At the foot of a flight of steps leading to a cabin higher up the dark wall of the gulch, they both halted and stood listening a moment. Some of the night sounds of Morgantown reached them here; but mostly there was stillness, broken only by the strengthening night wind that brought a hint, even on a mild June evening, of the chill of the higher peaks. From where they stood, most of Morgantown lay below, its lights scattered and spilling helter-skelter down the throat of the gulch.

Laying her hand on the old man's sleeve, Stella Harbord said, "Thank you, Sam, for taking the trouble to walk me home."

"What trouble?" the lawman grunted. "I got my evening rounds to make; I don't usually make 'em in the company of a handsome young woman."

"Oh, go along with you!" she scolded, in mock severity. He chuckled a little and the next moment winced, abruptly shifting weight off his left leg, at a stab of pain that was rather more severe than usual. She knew him well, and must have guessed something; for she asked, "Is it bothering you, Sam?"

"Who, me?" the old man retorted. "Oh, hell no. I'm fine—fine as frog's hair."

5

If she doubted him she was kind enough not to say so; nevertheless, he was grateful that she didn't ask him to tackle that steep rise of wooden steps to her cabin. She took the package he had carried home for her, and told him, "Well, goodnight, Sam. And thank you again."

"Anytime at all. But maybe tomorrow you'll finally get those books to balance, and won't have to stay late at the store another night." He hesitated, not sure whether he should say more; but he knew she needed encouragement and he added earnestly, "And—who knows? Maybe tomorrow you'll hear something."

She was silent a long moment; then he heard her sigh. "Sam," she said in a small voice, "I try hard not to worry; but it's with me every minute—and this time for almost a month, since he wrote me from Silver Hill. I wake up at night and lie there wondering where he is, and what can be happening to him. I so much long to hear— and yet I know, too, the risk it is for Jim to post a letter, or pick up one from me . . . Oh, Sam! I just don't know! When I think that it could go on this way, perhaps for years—!"

The old lawman patted her arm. "You're a brave girl, Stella," he said. "I know you own the courage to do what you have to." He added heavily, "Well, I got doors to check. I better get on with it."

"Goodnight, Sam," she said again. "I'll see you tomorrow."

But as she started up the steps, Sam White still made no move to set about his nightly routine. That damned left leg was bothering him, worse than he'd have wanted Stella Harbord to know; the bullet wound from last autumn had supposedly healed, but in his heart he suspected he was growing just too damned old to sustain that kind of damage and get over it, the way a younger man would do.

Suddenly he was feeling weary. He thought of the hour ahead, and his town marshal's duty of going the rounds of the business houses to check doors and windows and make certain all was quiet and in order; and he told himself it would be only sensible to rest that aching leg a bit before continuing. So he let himself down onto the bottom step and absently kneaded the ache in his thigh while he sat there contemplating the darkness and the high mesh of stars, and faced the unvoiced question: Just how long could he continue to fill this job of carrying the badge in Morgantown? Was it, maybe, time for him to quit?

Absentmindedly he had dug his old briar out of waistcoat pocket; he put the pipe in his mouth without loading it and sucked thoughtfully at the bit, as he listened to Stella Harbord climbing the steps to her porch.

The merchants of Morgantown kept their places of business locked tight after hours, but few people bothered about doing the same to their houses. Stella had thought once or twice of putting a padlock on her door but there was little enough in the tiny, three-room structure to tempt a thief, and it went against the grain of a Westerner's attitudes. So now she merely had to lift the latch, step inside and close the door behind her. It was only afterward that she halted, suddenly frowning into the room's darkness.

Her eyes adjusted and the two windows became gray rectangles, giving her her bearings. Something, somewhere, was wrong—she seemed unable to put a name to it. Puzzled and vaguely apprehensive, she moved to the room's center and set down her package on the table, while she felt around for the box of matches, got one out and struck it alight. Waiting until the flame caught and held steady, with her other hand she lifted the chimney from the kerosene tablelamp—and caught her breath as she realized the glass under her fingers was already warm.

Instantly she recognized what had struck her as wrong the moment she entered: a faint tang of burnt kerosene hanging in the air, from the extinguished lamp. She had had no time to do more than register this, when the man was on her.

A hand clamped itself over her mouth to prevent her crying out, another came around to close upon her own hand, which still held the flickering match. In her ear a gruff voice—oddly muffled, as though behind cloth—gave someone an order: "Take that chimney from her before she drops it!"

Her head was clamped too tightly for her to do more than glimpse the second man, who appeared at the edge of her vision and took the glass from unresisting fingers. Now the voice behind her said, "Go on—light the lamp!" The hand, its fingers backed by dark fur, squeezed down on her own so that she could not have opened them to drop the burning match. The flame was already getting uncomfortably warm as she watched, helpless, while her hand was directed toward the exposed wick and held there until the flame caught.

Only after the second man replaced the chimney, and the lamp's flickering light settled, was she freed and the hand removed from her face. She jerked away, struck the table's edge and caught at it to steady herself. She put her scorched fingers to her mouth as she braced herself, staring at her captors. The voice said, "Now we can talk business. . . ."

Both were masked, with handkerchiefs drawn tight across their faces and shapeless hats pulled low, but to her they had very much the look of range tramps. Their jeans and boots looked worn and the jacket of one was actually split open at the shoulder. They wore gunbelts, however, and the one who had held her prisoner now had a gun trained on her. Too angry to be frightened just yet, she demanded stoutly, "Who are you? What do you want with me?"

"Who we are don't signify," replied the voice she had heard before. "And we ain' t here to hurt you. But we want information, and if you know what's good for you you'll tell us what we want to know.

"Where's Bannister?"

She understood, then, and felt herself turn cold. But she gave no answer, and at this the man appeared to lose his temper. He stepped nearer; suddenly he had her by an arm, and was shaking her so that her head snapped upon her neck. "Come on, lady!" he gritted. "Don't try holding out on us! Jim Bannister is fair game. He's wanted for hanging—and we got as much right as anybody, to that twelve thousand in syndicate money he carries on his head."

The other man chimed in. He seemed considerably younger than his companion, so much so that his high-pitched voice threatened to crack with keyed-up tension. "And you know where he is! You're his woman—we heard that more than once since we hit this town, from people that claimed to know."

Lamplight gleamed from the barrel of the gun. "Either you talk, or—"

"You'd use that on me?" she retorted. She knew it was foolhardy, trying to defy two armed men; but it was not in her to show a hint of fear.

The one who held her arm said tightly, "Anybody that comes between me and twelve thousand dollars—"

He broke off as, without warning, Stella Harbord suddenly stepped in closer and tried for his face with her free hand. Her nails found flesh, raking down across a cheek, pulling the mask free. The effect was startling. The man stumbled back, his hold broken; a chair got in his way and he knocked it over, stumbled and went to the floor with it. The gun must have been jarred out of his hand. It was sent spinning and, as it struck the wall, went off with a report that was ear-splitting, within the confines of the tiny living room.

But though one man was down, his younger companion was there and he grabbed at Stella. She fought desperately, in every way she could. When he caught one fist, she struck him with the other and knocked the battered hat off his head; lank, tawny hair spilled down over his sweating forehead. When he managed to trap that hand, too, she began kicking and heard him pant curses behind his mask. He was trying to crowd her back against the table, immobilize and subdue her there. By this time the bigger man was on his feet again, yelling instructions: "Goddamn wildcat! *Hold* her!" while he tried to circle, get in where he could lend help.

And in that instant, boots struck the porch outside.

The door flung open. Stella was unable to get a look at the man who stood framed there, but she heard Sam White's shout. "Stella! *Drop!*" She obeyed instantly, allowing her body to go limp and letting her weight carry her to the floor. The man who held her wrists was pulled off balance and had to let her go; as he straightened, Sam White's revolver opened up from the doorway.

Though the bullet apparently missed, the fellow exclaimed, "Oh, Christ!" in a voice almost like a frightened boy's. Next moment he stumbled across Stella Harbord, where she huddled against the floor making herself as small as possible; she saw that his companion had given him a violent shove out of the way, and now was plunging past him and through the door of the kitchen leanto, leaving his gun behind, where it had fallen.

Sam White yelled something and started forward, but after a single step his left knee buckled under him and he went down, heavily. He staggered up again almost at once, but by that time both of Stella's attackers had vanished, the second one on the heels of the first. Dazed, she watched Sam go charging in pursuit, heard him cross the kitchen at a limping run and plunge through the back door, into the night.

Out back, there was a gunshot—another. Afterward, however much she strained to listen she could hear nothing at all.

She scrambled and, gathering her skirt, made her way through the kitchen to the door, which had been left open; there, reaction hit her and she had to catch at the doorframe just a moment, for support. The wall of the gulch rose sharply just outside the door, toward a black sky swimming in stars. On the left, where brush grew thick, Stella thought she heard someone floundering away in a reckless smashing of broken branches.

By the time these noises had faded, her eyes had adjusted to the dark and she made out a figure lying motionless on the ground. Giving a cry of alarm, she fell to her knees beside her friend.

The old man stirred, swore painfully. "I ain't shot," he reassured her. "Just that bum leg, giving out—I took them stairs too fast, I guess, when I heard a gun go off inside your cabin." He pushed up to a sitting position; he still had his own weapon and he said with some satisfaction, as he peered into the night, "I think I maybe done some damage to one of them. They hurt *you,* girl?" he demanded.

"No, no," she answered quickly. "I don't think that was the idea. They wanted information. I thought one of them was hardly more than a boy—and frightened."

"Couple of amateurs!" the old marshal said sourly. "I don't reckon they'll be back." Nor did the brief sound of gunfire seem to have roused any alarm, in the quiet June night—it would take more than that to cause any real disturbance in a community like Morgantown. "Could you give me a hand up?" Sam White grunted. With her aid he got stiffly onto his feet, and they went back to the house.

Still shaken from her experience, Stella tried to put her tumbled hair to rights as she looked about her with time to see, now, what the intruders had done. The living room, and the bedroom too, had been thoroughly ransacked; drawers stood open, their contents plowed through and scattered. The few books on her shelf looked as though someone had riffled through their pages and tossed them aside. She shook her head in angry exasperation.

Sam White had righted the fallen chair and let himself into it, laying his gun on the table. He was kneading the hurt leg, grimacing as he probed the soreness of recently healed tissues; but he waved the woman aside when she would have done something to help him. "I'll be all right," he told her gruffly. "Leg just ain't ready yet for that much exercise, all at once. But it does make you mad, to have your body let you down. You begin to realize you're just too damn old!"

"You're not that old, Sam," the woman said.

"The bullet you took—in line of duty—would slow anyone up. And there's not a person in Morgantown who doesn't understand."

The marshal shrugged, as though he lacked the will to argue. He gestured toward a corner of the room. "I see one of 'em lost his gun." Stella went and got it for him—a plain, rubber-butted revolver, still giving off the reek of exploded powder. Looking at her with pure respect in his faded eyes, he said, "I'll wager they're still wondering what they tangled with. You must really have given 'em a fight!"

"Sam . . ." With sudden determination she drew up a chair opposite, placed her hands on the table's edge; she spoke solemnly and earnestly, watching his expression in the lamplight that fell on both their faces. "Sam, I've known for some time I was going to have to make a decision. It looks as though—tonight—it's been made for me. I've got to leave Morgantown."

"Leave?" he echoed, frowning. "This is your home! You've made a place here for yourself."

"And I like the town, and most of its people. I don't *want* to go. But I no longer have a choice." She hesitated. "I hadn't told you before—this isn't the first time someone's broken in here. The other time, I wasn't absolutely sure," she went on as the old man stared at her. "It was not quite two weeks ago. I came home from the store, and was almost certain someone had been searching the place—there were drawers that were not quite the way I remembered leaving them, other little signs. But I didn't want to believe it, and so I managed not to—for a while.

"There's no doubt of it any longer," she went on, "because now it's happened twice—and it will again. Sam, I'm a marked person! As time goes on, more and more men, as desperate as those two tonight, will be coming here, certain that I'm the key to help them lay hands on Jim Bannister and collect that awful reward."

"Was that what they were after—a line on Bannister?"

She nodded. "It's exactly what they were after. First, they ransacked the place, looking for heaven knows what . . . letters, I suppose, that might give them some kind of clue. When they didn't find anything, they put out the lamp and waited in the dark for me to come home, so they could grab me and force me to tell them what they wanted to know. It was just by chance you were on hand to stop them."

Suddenly she was trembling, uncontrollably. Sam reached across the table to place his hand on hers. "Now that it's happened," he pointed out soothingly, "don't you see, there are things we can do to make sure it never happens again."

"We can't ever be sure! Besides, it isn't fair to you. After all, you *are* the law. What will happen if people get the notion *you* know something

16

about Jim Bannister's whereabouts, and are doing nothing about it?"

"Let me worry about that," he answered firmly. "My conscience is clear. I don't know where Bannister is—but I also know he isn't any murderer and that he has to stay free, if he's to have any chance to get a reversal of that New Mexico conviction. I'm well aware you have ways of getting in touch with him, but I prefer not to make that any of my business. And if anybody wants my badge for it, they're just about damn welcome!"

"Even so, it would be better all around if I weren't here, to be a temptation for those reward hunters. I honestly don't think I could go through, again, what happened tonight—because, what terrifies me is the thought that they might actually force me to betray him. You know, I'm not the strongest person in the world!"

"You're strong enough," Sam White assured her; but then he added heavily, "I guess, though, you know your own mind—much as I'll hate to see you gone. When will you leave?"

"The sooner the better, I'm afraid. I'll have to give Mr. Canby notice, at the store, and crate whatever I want sent where I'm going. I've been thinking about San Francisco—I was never there, but it should be a large enough place for me to lose myself, and for Jim's enemies not be able to trace me."

Sam White sighed heavily and got to his feet. "You know your own mind," he said, "and at that, I ain't sure but what you're right. Word is out that Bannister's here in Colorado, and this part of the country's getting altogether too hot for him. Likely the state's never seen such an influx of manhunters, professionals and amateurs both— all of them dead set on the twelve-thousand-dollar bounty.

"It's my thought he'll never be persuaded to leave for some place safe, not as long as you're here; but if he knew you'd taken off for distant parts, he might follow. Frankly, I don't know any other thing that would jar him loose—and I have to say, it would be the best thing for him."

Stella nodded thoughtfully. "I really hadn't thought of that. I wonder if you could be right. . . ."

"It's worth thinking about."

He stood looking down at her, the lamplight finding copper glints in her brown hair, softening the line of her cheek and the gravely troubled cast of her lips; and he had to admit that in spite of everything Jim Bannister must be counted a lucky man, to have the regard of someone like Stella Harbord. Well, they both had been hurt— Bannister by the forces of law and the ruthless power of an Eastern syndicate, Stella Harbord seeing her husband dead at the hands of an angry lynch mob. But that made all the more valuable

18

the mutual feeling those two had discovered. And by God, they deserved better than the world had given them!

Sam pointed to the captured revolver he had left lying on the table, and said gruffly, "You best keep that handy, in case our friends should show again—though I strongly doubt it. I'll keep an eye out for them while I go my rounds; and I'll be dropping in again later, to make sure you're all right."

"I'm sure I will be," she said, smiling at the gruff earnestness of his manner. "I'll take care, all the same. And don't *you* put too much on that hurt leg of yours, you hear?"

"I hear," he said, white mustache lifting to his grin, and left her.

CHAPTER II

The coach had been climbing steadily, ever since the noon stop. At first he was conscious of the pressure of the seat back against his spine; after a while he noticed that the passengers facing him seemed to be having some trouble bracing themselves to keep from sliding into his lap. It was only later that he became aware they had lifted into thicker stands of timber, and that the driver on the box was making more use of his whip, shouting at his teams to hold them in the collars.

Even then, it could be a little startling when a turn in the road suddenly opened a view of a canyon dropping away below him, and he saw the ranked spires of tall treeheads marching away, more or less at his own eye level. . . .

Stella Harbord, after a night and now a second day of sitting bolt upright and braced to the lurching of the clumsy stagecoach, felt she had come very near to exhaustion; but now she sat suddenly straighter to get a better view and catch the pungent tang of sun-warmed pine needles, her discomfort for that moment forgotten. There was no comment from any of her fellow travelers—as the only woman among the four inside passengers, she'd insulated herself against their attention but by now they appeared indifferent to her, or to anything but their own discomfort. Even the paunchy cattle buyer seated next to Stella, who had been trying unsuccessfully to make conversation ever since the stage left Morgantown, was sunk in an unthinking, uncaring misery—head bobbing, eyes closed and raddled cheeks haggard with weariness.

Just one of these men seemed to have an interest in the scenery. He looked to be bearing up well enough, though he'd been on the coach with her when it left Morgantown and, for all she knew, might have come farther than that. She had found herself studying him, idly—something about the man intrigued her, probably because he didn't fit any of the types she was familiar with. She hadn't the slightest idea who he might be. His skin was sun-darkened but he didn't have the rough-worn look of a cattleman. He wore a brown corduroy jacket with leather patches at the elbows, California pants and polished boots; a narrow-brimmed hat sat precisely above his narrow face. His hair was dark but salted with gray, his eyes jet black; he had a way of definitely looking at something until he seemed to absorb what he wanted from it, dismiss it and pass on.

Seated opposite Stella, he was looking out the window but recently he seemed aware of her look resting on him and turned his head, those black eyes meeting hers coolly and without expression.

21

Something about them made her uncomfortable. They were, she thought suddenly, the coldest eyes she'd ever seen.

Now the way began to climb in earnest toward the sheer wall of the Rockies, and sometime in midafternoon they tooled up before a station that was little more than a hovel built of log and stone, with a corral and leanto barn and dense fir closing it in. As the driver swung down from his perch and passed the window Stella asked dubiously, "Do we have a meal here?"

"No, ma'am," he told her. "That won't be till the home station at Ute Springs. We stay here just long enough to hitch on fresh teams, before we tackle the pass."

Within minutes they were away again, the road lifting by steep switchbacks, the horses laboring under the whip. Progress slowed to a crawl. The shouldering ranks of timber thinned and gave way to barren rock as they rose above timberline. And then, abruptly, they were on top of the world.

Here they pulled up to rest the horses, and the travelers got out for a better view from this point atop the continent's spine. Stella felt almost as though she stood at the edge of a table. Behind her rose even higher peaks, glistening with granite; but at her feet the land dropped away in folds furred dark with timber, showing the blue glint of lakes and the flash of tumbling water catching the sun. Her lungs reached for the thinner air at this altitude; she felt the pumping of her heart at even the slightest exertion. But it was the mere bigness of the scene spread before her that left her stunned.

"Quite a view . . ."

She turned, realizing the words were directed at her. The cold-eyed stranger had come up beside her. He had a cigar that he had taken from a coat pocket; now he snapped a match and put the flame to it, behind a palm that shielded it from the steady wind. Through a spurt of blue smoke, his eyes regarded her face.

Just now Stella was too awed by emotion to do anything but agree. "Tremendous!" she exclaimed.

"Almost worth the punishment we're taking." The match was dropped and he set a boot on it. He drew deeply at the cigar, savoring it. She felt his eyes on her as he casually added, "You're traveling far?"

She looked at him quickly. His face showed nothing, but the question itself put her on her guard.

"To the railroad." She let him see her frown as she gave the least-inviting answer she could think of. A moment later she moved away slightly, as though seeking a better view. She had an idea he might follow, but whether or not he took it as a rebuff he seemed to accept the hint; he let her go.

When the whip called for his passengers to load

23

up, it was the paunchy cattle buyer who gave Stella a hand up into the coach; the man with the cigar had hung back, as though to enjoy his smoke to the last possible moment. The driver yelled again, and he simply flipped the unfinished cigar away and returned without hurry to his place. He had barely swung the door closed when a shout from the box sent the rested team into their collars, and the coach jerked into motion.

The cattle buyer seemed to think he had managed an opening and he launched at once into a monologue, giving Stella to know that he was a man of wide travel and experience. She answered a time or two, in monosyllables, and at last deliberately turned her attention to the window. With only her back to talk to, the buyer finally gave up and lapsed into surly silence.

Stella Harbord caught the cold-eyed man looking at her, and wondered if there was a faint expression of amusement at seeing still another stranger being put in his place. Up on the box, the driver was riding his brake to hold back the heavy coach and keep it from running down the horses; they took the steep curves spilling down from the high pass, with Ute Springs station waiting at the end of this leg of the run.

In the trees some dozen yards behind Jim Bannister, his dun horse stirred restlessly. At once he dropped the glasses he had been using and, rolling aside into denser shadow, drew his gun. Crouched there, he held his breath while he searched the brush and timber, looking for whatever had disturbed the horse.

There was only stillness, a deceptive stirring of air along the hillside, and once or twice a jay scolding somewhere. The dun stood like a statue, its head lifted and twisted about to peer fixedly at some point in the thick growth. Bannister could see nothing there to alarm it, and after a long minute the dun lowered its head again and began once more cropping at the thin stand of grass where it had been tied.

Bannister slowly let the trapped breath from his lungs.

He stayed as he was for another five minutes, however, until he was absolutely sure. At last convinced there was no enemy working up to try and catch him without warning, he put the gun away and turned again to his study of the stage station layout below him.

For the better part of two hours he had kept a watch on the buildings and corrals, moving to a new position whenever he felt he had been too long in one spot where some inadvertent glint of sun on the lenses of his field glasses might have given him away. With the dun at his back to act as a watchdog, he felt reasonably safe while he put his attention on memorizing the layout of the station, and checking its occupants. There were three, he had decided—the station tender himself and a woman, perhaps his wife, and a handyman who was busy this afternoon working around the barn. Otherwise the only life he could see was the half dozen horses, replacements for the stage teams, moving about in the corral, and a spotted hound that had collapsed in the dust by the station doorway and lain there ever since as though it were dead.

Day's end was drawing close. A blue column of woodsmoke had begun to lift from the stone chimney, brought so near by the glasses that he could almost imagine he was able to smell it. The woman was probably starting up preparations to feed the passengers expected in on the afternoon stage, and the thought reminded Bannister uncomfortably of his own empty stomach. His saddle rations were all but exhausted, and in his touch-and-go existence it was always a question when he could expect to replenish them.

That problem would have to wait. Right now he was concerned only with the purpose that had brought him here—and with the impatience that, for the first time since he commenced his vigil, began to stir in him as he saw evening shadows lengthening.

The stage road lay empty, where it curved into view around a shoulder of rock and looped past the stage station and then out of sight again, swallowed up in lower timber. Once the station agent came out and stood a moment gazing up the road, as though he too wondered where the coach was. The spotted hound lumbered to its feet, scratched its ear with a hind foot, went trotting out of sight behind the stable. There was lamplight now in the station windows, as sunlight leaked out of this hollow, even though the peaks above it still held sunlight and a few clouds glowed warmly in a pale sky.

Suddenly Bannister's head jerked up as something caught the corner of his eye. He brought up the glasses and tried to focus on it.

On the mountain wall facing him, beyond the stage road at its base, a stain of dust rising out of the trees had been touched to gold by the setting sun. He watched that gilded banner and saw it dip lower, descending at an angle down the timbered mountain face; he couldn't see yet what caused it, but it gave the first hint of something he had not even suspected: There must be a trail of sorts, yonder, that climbed the wall under its thick growth of fir and pine.

Presently the dust was swallowed and lost in the shadows. Still Bannister kept the glasses searching and presently, sure enough, a pair of horsemen broke out of the lower timber and came on at a leisurely pace toward the station buildings. He studied them as best he could in the gathering dusk, but could tell only that one rode a sorrel, the other a brown. They rode from sight behind the station and apparently tied their mounts. A minute later they were back, on foot, the hound trailing them as they approached the open door. Lamplight silhouetted them briefly as they entered.

Bannister puzzled over them, for some minutes, wondering about that trail down the mountain—and where it might head to. He couldn't imagine; its existence had come as a total surprise to him.

A moment later it was put completely out of his mind. Heralded by a brief, spattering echo of hoofs and turning wheels and slamming timbers, the stage came swinging into view behind its six-horse hitch. The coach lamps had been lighted and he watched them, tiny spots of brightness swinging against the dark mountain's face as they drew in toward the station. Down there, the barnman came carrying a lighted lantern that spread a swaying circle. The dog was there too, running about excitedly as though it never had seen a stage arriving before; the man finally gave it a kick with his boot that sent it scampering.

Now the stage came rolling to a halt, in the open-work area before the station. The horses stomped and settled; the driver and another man—shotgun guard or outside passenger—clambered off the forward boot. But Jim Bannister kept his glasses focused on the closed door of the coach, unconsciously holding his breath as he waited.

The door was opened from the inside and a man backed out, then reached up to help someone. Bannister glimpsed a gray traveling skirt, and after that the woman was down and he cleared his lungs in a single explosive grunt, all the tensions of his long wait broken and falling from him as, even in the dim light of the station yard, he recognized her. He paid little mind to the other passengers after that, all his attention was on Stella Harbord.

He saw how she paused and looked around her, as though studying the darkness outside that one center of lamplight and activity. For a moment she seemed to stare directly into the lens of the glasses, and Jim Bannister felt almost that he could speak to her.

Then she turned and followed the others into the station; and Bannister, his vigil at last ended, rose at once from behind the log where he had been lying, and returned to the waiting dun.

The glasses went into a case strapped to his saddle pommel. He tightened the cinch, jerked the reins free of the pine branch where he had anchored them, and swung astride. He was a big, yellow-haired man, this Jim Bannister—a head taller than most, and with a frame to match. It made him a natural target, all too easy for someone to notice and remember even without having heard a description, or seen one of the syndicate's reward notices. Even in a completely strange place, he could never be completely sure of going unrecognized.

Now he took a circuitous route down from the hill and across the wooded hollow toward the buildings, around the snow-fed trickle of water that gave Ute Springs its name. Stars were beginning to appear, but no moon as yet; the going remained pitch black and treacherous, and he had to let the dun pick its way.

He gained the stage road some distance above the station, crossed it and went into the fringe of timber beyond, to make his cautious approach to the station yard. When he had come near enough he pulled rein and, placing the heels of both cupped hands to his lips, sent a good imitation of an owl's hoot through the stillness. After a moment he repeated it, and then he waited.

For a spell, nothing happened. Then the woman appeared, alone, in the station doorway. She hesitated a moment, and afterward went directly to the waiting coach; opening the door, she reached inside for a reticule she had left on the seat— her excuse, apparently, for coming outside. She stood holding it, looking about her uncertainly.

Once more Bannister repeated the signal— softly, giving her direction. Stella checked the station again with an anxious glance. Deciding she wasn't being observed, she tossed the reticule back into the coach and a moment later was coming toward him. Bannister dismounted, calling softly, "This way . . ." She veered to the sound of his voice, and was in his arms.

Though she was tall for a woman, Bannister had to bend his head to meet her kiss. She clung to him fiercely, and then laid her head against his chest; his fingers touched her cheek and found the warm wetness of tears. "Here, now!" he chided gently.

"I'm sorry!" she breathed. "I've counted the hours and the days and the weeks. So many nights I've lain awake, wondering where you were and what could be happening to you!"

"Well, I guess you can see I'm all right."

"Oh, yes. And thank God for that!" She clung more tightly, and he could feel her trembling. Bannister continued to hold her for a moment, while the trees rocked slightly overhead. Though his awareness was all of the woman in his arms, some disciplined part of his mind was busily probing the silence, testing every sound, wary of danger.

After a moment he said quietly, "And so, you're leaving me . . ."

She released herself so that she could peer into his face, though it was really too dark for that. "You don't think I *want* to!"

"Of course I don't," he assured her. "You explained your reasons, and you're perfectly right. It's plain, too many people have found out about us—which makes it too risky for you. Men who

31

smell a reward aren't particular who they hurt."

"I was so afraid, as usual, my letter wouldn't reach you. At every station since I left Morgantown, I've watched for you—hardly daring to hope."

Bannister smiled. "Did you think I'd let you go without managing somehow?"

"But I knew the danger. Jim—" She hesitated, as though summoning her arguments; and as she did so he turned his head sharply, not certain that he hadn't heard something back in the timber— the snap of a twig, perhaps. It wasn't repeated, and then the woman was saying earnestly, "You won't come with me?"

"To California?" Bannister shook his head. "I just can't do that—not now."

"But with every day that passes there's bound to be more men combing these hills for you, trying for that twelve thousand dollars. Why should you wait and let them close in? I don't understand!"

Bannister said, "I'll try to explain. That syndicate man I had to kill, down in New Mexico—that fellow McGraw: I've learned that at one time he had a mistress. They split up, and the word is she was last known to be somewhere here in Colorado. She may be here yet."

"I see," Stella said quietly.

"By locating her, and getting her to talk, I might be able to learn more details about McGraw's work for the syndicate—maybe, even, something to back my claim that I was justified in killing him. I know it's only an outside chance, but everything depends on following any possible lead."

There was a silence while she absorbed this. "And if you don't find this woman?" she said then. "Or manage to get anything useful from her?"

Bannister lifted a shoulder. "Eventually I suppose I'm going to have to admit that I've lost. Some day, maybe. Only, I'm not quite ready to spend the rest of my life in exile, somewhere like South America."

"I'd go with you."

"I know you would. And if it comes to that, I'll ask you. But—not yet."

Standing close to him, she put up a hand and ran her fingers gently down the lean plane of his cheek—spare of flesh after these months of constant running from the law, stubbled now with a day's growth of wiry yellow beard.

"Jim . . ." But she let the word trail off, as though there were really suddenly nothing more to say.

"You'd better get back," he told her gruffly. "They'll be wondering where you've got to. They might even come looking . . ."

That was when the voice spoke from the shadows: "Stay where you are! Both of you. Bannister, this is where it ends."

CHAPTER III

Jim Bannister went very still, hearing Stella's sharp intake of breath, mindful of her close beside him and never for a moment doubting that the voice had the authority of a drawn gun behind it. Very carefully, turning nothing but his head, he looked around and picked out the shape of the man who stood a dozen feet away, only his face and hands palely visible in the tree shadows.

And the glint of metal . . .

"Both of you stand easy," the voice said. "Keep your hands in sight, Bannister. Now you, Ma'am—I want you to take the gun from his holster and toss it to me. But I warn you: Make one false move, Mrs. Harbord, and I'll shoot *him*. He's big enough, he should be an easy target."

Bannister felt her stiffen, on hearing her name. He suspected she had recognized the voice, for now she exclaimed, "Then you knew, all along, who I was?"

"Why, naturally. I had my eye on you for some time. When it became clear you were getting ready to leave Morgantown, I was pretty sure you'd have arranged to meet this man somewhere along the line."

"And all you had to do was buy a ticket on the

same coach!" Stella's voice was bitter. "I never suspected anything—not even when you spoke to me, up at the pass. I led you straight to him!"

"I'm afraid that's right." He added, "The gun, Mrs. Harbord . . ."

Bannister warned her, "Do what he says."

He himself was helpless, with the woman there to be in danger if his captor should be tempted to shoot. He stood motionless and felt his holster lightened as she lifted the sixshooter from it. "Over here," the man ordered. "But, easy! We don't want it to go off." She complied by stooping and placing the weapon on the ground, then giving it a push with her foot across the grass and pine-needle litter. The man swiftly scooped it up and shoved it behind his belt, under the skirt of his coat.

All the while his own drawn gun never left its target on Bannister's chest. Even in the dim starlight there seemed something infinitely cold about the narrow face, and shadowed eyes.

Stella demanded suddenly, "Who *are* you?"

"The name is Dodd, Mrs. Harbord." He sounded half amused at her question.

"Are you the law?"

"No, I wouldn't say that. Not exactly."

Bannister spoke crisply, able now to supply the answer. "He's a professional bounty hunter, Stella. His name is Wes Dodd, and he was at one time a deputy United States Marshal for the

35

Colorado district; but perhaps the pay wasn't as good as what he could make collecting reward money—or maybe he felt hampered working inside the law, where a man has to show restraint in using a gun. So, he turned in his marshal's badge and went on his own. From what I hear, he's made a profitable thing out of it. "

"Well!" the other man said heavily. "You seem to know all about me."

"It's my business to know about men like you."

"Then I hope you know not to take any foolish chances!" Dodd reached into a pocket of his coat; there was a clink of metal as he stepped forward. "Put out your wrists."

For just a moment, Bannister considered refusing. But the revolver muzzle trained on him put a knot of ice in his middle; the price on him was collectible whether delivered alive or dead, and he knew it would make absolutely no difference to Wes Dodd whether or not he pulled the trigger. Slowly, Bannister forced himself to extend both hands. There was a quick movement, and the chill of steel snapped into place about each wrist, in turn. Dodd gave the handcuffs a tug, roughly testing them; then he stepped back, as though wary even now about being in too close reach of his prisoner.

"That's strictly on good behavior," he warned. "Give me any trouble, Bannister, and you'll have those arms shackled behind your back—a good deal more uncomfortable. Have you eaten?" he added gruffly.

"No."

"Well, I hadn't finished, myself. So, we'll just walk over to the station now—and we'll do it carefully and easy. You, too, ma'am," he told Stella. "You both walk ahead of me. I'll fetch the horse."

A gesture of the gun barrel motioned them forward. Stella fell in beside Bannister, and as they started toward the buildings, crossing the ruts of the stage road, they heard Wes Dodd following and the thud of the dun's hoofs, at lead.

Stella stumbled a time or two on the uneven ground. Jim Bannister could hear her crying, and felt her hand close tight upon his wrist and on the cold steel that encircled it. "I'll never forgive myself!" she said brokenly. "I thought I was protecting you—and instead I put you right into his hands!"

"You had no way of knowing," he said. "Don't blame yourself." But he knew he could do little to combat the hopeless guilt she was feeling; he only hoped he'd managed to keep despair from showing in his own voice. For his part, the touch of the handcuffs had been enough to start a cold sweat—it was like a renewal of nightmare, reviving all the grim horror he'd known in months of imprisonment and trial, and then standing in irons before a jury and hearing himself condemned to hang. . . .

In silence they entered the station yard where the coach stood with its lamps still burning. Squares of yellow light spilled from the windows and open doorway of the station, and there were the voices inside and the sounds and smells of dinner in progress. Despite his predicament, Bannister felt the saliva start as he was reminded of the hours since he last ate.

"Hold it!" Wes Dodd ordered. They waited while he looped the dun's reins to a hitching rack near the entrance and, having holstered his handgun, slid Jim Bannister's rifle from its place in the saddle boot. Bannister had his first look at the man who had captured him. The lean, tight-lipped face impressed him as that of someone competent, dangerous, and probably without any scruples at all—an estimate that accorded with what he had heard about this lawman turned bounty killer. There would be no mercy here, and no carelessness.

The cold eyes rested on him, measuring him in turn. Wes Dodd nodded. "Very well," he said crisply, and pointed with the rifle muzzle. "Inside . . ."

The station's interior was crude enough. Outside, the mountain chill was descending as night deepened, but here doors and windows stood open against the heat of the big woodburning range that dominated the kitchen end of the one main room. At its other end was a plain counter, with another door behind it that Bannister supposed led to the proprietor's sleeping quarters.

Most of the room's space was filled by a long table, flanked by benches; a half dozen diners, all of them men, were noisily busy at their meal in a hum of talk and clatter of dishes and cheap utensils. This noise gradually died as the newcomers entered, and those facing the door saw Dodd's prisoner and the handcuffs on his wrists. Both talk and eating ceased; heads lifted and turned, and yonder at the stove a fat woman with her drab hair pulled into an untidy bun looked around and went motionless, a mixing spoon forgotten in her hand.

His own expression coldly unrevealing, Bannister met the curious looks that raked his big frame. He swiftly sorted out the men at the table, spotting the gnarled and weather-beaten driver and three others that he judged to be passengers from the stage. That left a pair in sweated range hats and well-worn denims— obviously, the two whose dust he'd watched, earlier, descending the mountain wall.

It was the station tender who broke the silence. "What is this?" he exclaimed. He was a gaunt fellow with a gleaming and hairless skull, who stood at the counter making pencil entries in a book, the spotted hound asleep at his feet. Putting down the pencil he demanded of Wes Dodd, "Just what are you bringing in here, mister?"

The manhunter rapped the table sharply with the barrel of Bannister's rifle, and let his icy stare range across the listening faces. "I'll say this once," he announced crisply, "and I expect you all to heed it. I'm an officer of the court"—a lie in itself, as Jim Bannister knew, Dodd no longer being in any sense connected with the law. "I've just arrested this man, and I'll be taking him on the stage with us. He's wanted for a serious crime; he probably won't stop at killing if he has a chance to escape. So I don't want anyone interfering with him in any way. Do you all understand?"

There were uneasy exchanges of looks around the table. Seemingly satisfied, Dodd motioned his prisoner to an empty place and Bannister took it, stepping across the long bench. To the station agent, Wes Dodd said, "There's a saddled horse tied out there, that the prisoner had with him when I made the capture. It would be best if you'll have somebody take the gear off him and put him up, until the law decides what should be done with him."

The bald-headed man merely returned his look but made no move. Stella, meanwhile, had silently taken the place at Jim Bannister's left, where a partly finished plate of food indicated she must have been sitting before going to answer his summons. Dodd now seated himself, on the other side of his prisoner, and leaned the rifle by his right elbow beyond Bannister's reach.

Farther along the table, the fat man with the look of a cattle buyer spoke up angrily. "If that man's as dangerous as you say he is, then I very much object. My ticket says nothing about traveling in the same coach with an outlaw!"

"You want to wait here for the next one?" Wes Dodd suggested calmly.

The man began to sputter. He appealed indignantly to the station tender. "Can he do this?"

"Stageline ain't partial," the bald-headed man said with a shrug, and picked up his pencil. "Long as somebody pays his fare." That seemed to settle the matter, and at a word from Dodd a platter of steaks, and bowls of watery boiled potatoes and other victuals, began to move down the board.

In spite of his predicament, Jim Bannister was enough of an opportunist to know he had better eat while he had a chance. With manacled hands he couldn't hold the serving dishes and fill his plate at the same time, so Stella silently helped him. Her own hands trembled and once when their fingers met he found hers cold to the touch; but there was nothing useful he could think of to say to her.

Directly across the table, the two who had ridden down the mountain were watching him with open curiosity. They looked fairly young, and near enough in appearance to be obviously related—both stringily built, with the same dishfaced cast to their features, the same bony foreheads and hollow cheeks and prominent lantern jaws. The smaller, who had pale eyes and untrimmed reddish hair that he wore pushed back across his shoulders out of the way, watched the prisoner awkwardly maneuvering knife and fork. Presently he turned to his companion and said loudly, "Big sonofabitch, hain't he, Vern?"

"Damn right," the other answered—and their voices were alike, too, carrying a nasal sound that Bannister associated with certain hill regions of southern Missouri. "Oh, yeah, he stands out. What you say he's wanted for?" he demanded, turning to Wes Dodd.

The latter, methodically eating, gave him the briefest of looks. "I didn't say."

"Maybe there's even a little reward out for him?" the first one pointedly suggested, showing his teeth in a grin as he studied Bannister.

"What I'm thinking," commented the one named Vern, "he could be a problem for one man to handle. Now, reward money cain't mean anything to you," he pointed out to Dodd, "you bein' an officer an' all, not allowed by law to collect it. On the other hand, it's kind of remote from things where us Cagles live—ain't often the family comes by much in the way of foldin' money. And so, seein's it wouldn't cost you nothing, no reason me and Cousin Dewey couldn't pitch in and lend you a hand, takin' this big fellow wherever it is you want him took."

Dewey Cagle, wiping his mouth on the thumb of the hand that held his knife, eagerly agreed. "Why, hell yes! We'd figure it's the decent thing to do—lending the law a hand. And like Vern says, no sense lettin' a reward go wasted—assumin' there is one."

They eyed Dodd, waiting for an answer; but the latter, not bothering to answer, kept on with his eating. Taking it as a rebuff, the cousins exchanged a look and Dewey Cagle said, shrugging, "All right, mister, suit yourself. But, remember—we done offered." He eyed the prisoner darkly. "Damned if I ain't got a hunch the big feller's sitting there, right now, studyin' how to bust loose from you. Just *look* at him! If he gets away, though—hit's your affair, not our'n!"

And they both returned to wolfing their meals, seemingly unconcerned that the silent Wes Dodd hadn't been won over by their arguments.

Bannister had continued stolidly eating as though the talk had nothing to do with him. Actually he was sharply conscious of everything that went on about him, the slightest movement of the bounty hunter at his elbow. Jim Bannister's sixshooter was tucked behind the latter's belt, out of sight; his rifle leaned against the table on

Dodd's far side. The man wore no gun openly, but Bannister knew he had one under his coat, in a shoulder harness. Well armed as he was, Dodd couldn't be expected to pay much heed to Cagle's warning, or expect that he'd need any help getting his prisoner onto the stagecoach and to the nearest law office. Nor was there the least chance anyone else was going to have a look-in, collecting the syndicate's head money.

The other people in the room seemed almost to have forgotten the prisoner; talk resumed on other subjects as they finished up their meal, with the prospect of another miserable night of coach travel before them. The woman brought a fresh pot of coffee, steaming from the fire; when she refilled Bannister's cup he found it black with chicory and so hot that it burnt his tongue. He made a face and set the cup quickly down . . . and in that moment, knew suddenly what he was going to do.

It was desperate, and even barbaric, but better than no chance at all. Next to him Wes Dodd had just finished eating, dropping knife and fork into empty plate and pushing them away. There was no time really to think, or to warn Stella Harbord what he intended. Bannister's fingers tightened on his cup.

He spoke Dodd's name. And as the bounty hunter turned, Bannister let him have both cup and steaming contents, directly in the face.

CHAPTER IV

Wes Dodd cried out in surprise and pain, reeling and clapping both hands to his eyes as the blistering liquid struck. Everyone else at the table had been caught staring; of them all, Bannister doubted the stage passengers were armed but he thought the driver likely was. Also he was sure he'd glimpsed a holstered gun buckled high around the waist of Dewey Cagle, when the latter reached down the table to stab his fork into another chunk of beefsteak. And seeing that as the most likely point of danger, he was prepared.

He had already dropped both manacled hands to the table's edge. Now he levered sharply upward, toppling its heavy weight onto the men seated opposite. Dishes, food, cutlery spilled amid an outburst of startled yelling; in the same breath Bannister was turning to leap clear of the narrow bench behind him.

As he did he saw Stella's startled face and realized he couldn't leave her to the mercy of anyone like Dodd. He caught her arm, swept her up and set her on her feet. The room was all confusion and shouting, and frantic barking from the spotted dog that was almost hysterical now with excitement. Those pinned beneath the table were fighting to scramble free. Wes Dodd pawed at his eyes, momentarily blinded; the bald-pated proprietor remained motionless and staring behind his counter.

Bannister had won a moment's advantage, and knew he had to make the most of it. He couldn't hope to recover either of his weapons. Hurrying Stella ahead of him, he bolted instead for the door and gained the outer darkness. Where his horse stood tied to the hitching rack, he jerked the reins free, caught the horn with both manacled hands and leaped astride without touching stirrup. He leaned, seized Stella and hauled her up behind him.

"Hold on!" he grunted.

Her arms tightened about his waist, as a yank at the reins spun the horse and a kick of Bannister's heel sent it leaping forward. Iron shoes dug a gout of hard-packed dirt; and there was the big bulk of the stagecoach, looming directly in front of them. A quick maneuver avoided that obstacle, though the dun skidded on the turn and Bannister thought its rump barely missed colliding with one of the heavy wheels.

Then they were clear of it and plunging on, as yelling men came pouring belatedly through the station doorway.

A white disc of moon had just topped the timber-spired ridges to the east, spreading a milky gleam across the sky. Its glow made shadows blacker, rendered open spaces deceptive, turned the stage road into a ribbon looping dimly through the timber with the mountain wall rising hard above it. Behind them a gun slapped out two shots in hurried succession. Bannister felt the sweat break out on him at thought of the danger to Stella, but the shots were apparently wide, and they weren't repeated.

Instead he heard Vern Cagle's voice shouting orders: "Dewey! D'you hear? Bring up the horses!"

The stage road was under them now, and the dun horse wanted to turn into it. But Bannister, holding the animal steady, sent it straight across and into the black trees where he reined up briefly to get his bearings. "You all right?" he asked, over his shoulder, and heard what he took to be an affirmative. He told Stella, "Keep your head down," and kicked the dun forward.

They were held to a walk, now, as the animal picked its way through the close-growing trees. Low branches caught at them, slashing at his arms that he kept raised in an effort to protect his averted face. Stella pressed close, and when she spoke her anxious voice was muffled against his jacket: "Where are we going?"

"Riding double, they know we'd never outrun them," he answered. "And I haven't got a gun. We have to try something else . . ."

They were making too much noise themselves, smashing their way through brush and snapping brittle branches, to hear what might be going on behind them, but Bannister had little doubt pursuit had already started. Once he swore under his breath as the dun worked itself into a close-growing pocket of trees, had to be backed out and search another way. But then, abruptly, they seemed to break free and he was sure, even in near total darkness, he had found what he was looking for.

Halting, to half turn in the saddle as he tried to make out Stella's face, he asked, "You still in one piece?"

"I—think so," she answered, her voice sounding a trifle shaky. She had lost her hat, probably raked from her head by a passing limb; her hair was in disarray and fallen down from its pins, but she didn't seem much concerned about such things just then.

Bannister explained: "We've got a trail, here—I had to gamble on finding it. We didn't dare take the stage road, and there's no riding blind through that scrub timber. So it comes down to this."

"Where does the trail lead?"

"That's the trouble—I haven't the faintest idea. On the other hand, those Cagles do know: I only learned about it when I saw them riding it down to the station, earlier this evening. We can take it for granted they'll be after us. I think they've caught the smell of reward money!"

She said, "Then we'd better not waste time!"

"No." But still he hesitated, scowling over the black run of his thoughts; they tumbled out: "I hope it wasn't a mistake, dragging you away with me. But, Dodd is the kind who would use you as a hostage; I didn't dare leave you in his hands."

"You did right," she said. "Whatever happens I'd a thousand times rather be where you are. Surely you know that."

He slowly shook his head. "What's happening now is the very thing I've dreaded from the first moment I let myself get interested in you—and realized you felt the same way! All along I kept telling myself it would never happen, that I'd never have to drag you into danger."

"Don't say that!" she protested. "Whatever happens, I was the one led the trouble here. It was *my* fault. . . ." She laid a hand on his, impulsively, and he heard her catch her breath as she once again felt the cold touch of iron shackling his wrists. She said, "Is there any way to get rid of those?"

"There might be," he said, "if I had a file—or the key out of Wes Dodd's pocket! Since I don't have either one, I'll just have to put up with them." Abruptly, he shifted about in the saddle and again took the reins. "Hold tight," he said. "We're doing some climbing."

Her arms slipped again about his waist. He spoke to the dun, and sent it forward on this dimly marked trail.

• • •

In the station yard, the spotted dog was running in circles but the men were doing little but standing around and talking in great excitement, about the escape of the prisoner and his woman. Wes Dodd was beside himself, eyes still aflame and streaming tears as they made painful rainbow halos about the coach lamps, and about the white face of the new-risen moon. He located the station tender and his overalled barn helper and he descended on them, livid with fury and carrying Bannister's rifle clutched, forgotten, in one hand.

"Well, you see what's happened," he gritted. "If you'd put up that horse when I told you, those two wouldn't have escaped."

The bald-headed man had a grievance of his own. "I see what happened to my place of business! It's gonna take my woman all night to clean up the mess. You take a prisoner, you better make damn sure you got him!"

Dodd felt the angry heat mount to his cheeks but to argue now was a waste of time. "I'll need a horse," he snapped. "If you've got one that's broke to the saddle, I'll rent him—buy him— whatever. But I want him fast!"

The other merely looked at him. "Hell, I ain't running no livery stable. Only stock we carry belongs to the Company, and that ain't for public use."

"Are you forgetting? This is a law matter. . . ." But at that juncture the stage driver approached, breaking in on him.

"Gillis, I got a schedule to make and I can't do it standing around. Everybody's sure as hell through eating, so how about getting that fresh team hitched up?"

The bald-headed man said quickly, "Right away!" and gave his helper an elbow nudge. They turned and started for the barn, heedless of Wes Dodd's angry protest.

Someone said, with a chuckle, "Old man Gillis won't let you have no horse?"

He turned, irritably, to see one of the Cagles—the smaller one, who called himself Dewey—grinning as he came toward him leading a bony-looking sorrel by its reins. The saddle and gear were sorry looking, patched and strung together with odds and ends of rawhide and wire, but Dodd said quickly, "Maybe *you'll* make a deal. I'll give cash."

"For my bronc? You want to buy him?" Dewey Cagle shook his bony head. "Well, now, I don't think so."

"Damn it, don't you realize my prisoner's escaping!"

"If you remember, weuns offered once to lend you a hand with him," Cagle reminded him. "But you didn't want it none. Changed your tune a little, looks as if. And a mite late."

51

Exasperated, Dodd started to argue but was interrupted by the arrival of Vern Cagle, trotting up on a brown horse which seemed a match for his cousin's. He pulled rein with a heavy hand that caused the animal to throw up its head in protest. Dewey asked, "Anything?"

"Nothin' at all," the bigger man answered. "You?" When the other shook his head, Vern shrugged. "Well, there you are: They never could of tooken the stage road, either direction, without one or the other of us picking up the sign."

"Then where the devil *are* they?" Wes Dodd exploded. "Nobody can ride blind through country like this."

Vern looked down at him from the saddle. "Well, could be they've gone to cover somewhere, and in that case there won't be no diggin' 'em out till daylight. Still—I ain't so sure." He looked at his relative. "Are you of my mind in this, Cousin Dewey?"

"Reckon I am."

Vern turned again to the bounty hunter. "Weuns got us a hunch, mister. If we're right, could be you're in luck. Was you to decide hit might be worth something to you—"

Dodd got the drift, and he made an impatient gesture. "All right, all right! I'll pay you . . . fifty dollars apiece, to get my prisoner back."

He had thought, to look at them, fifty dollars would be a sizable sum to either of this pair; but he got no indication of it. Instead, something crafty came into their faces and Dewey Cagle asked pointedly, "How much for the woman?"

"Nothing at all for the woman. She's none of my concern. You get me Ban—" He checked himself. "Get me the man, and I don't care a damn what becomes of her."

He didn't miss the exchange of looks between the cousins. Stella Harbord was a damned handsome woman, and it had been a lucky inspiration throwing her in for bait. So, let the Cagles think about her—it might help take their minds off the man they would be hunting for, keep them from questioning whether he might be worth more than the fifty dollars they'd been promised. But after this, he had better guard against ever again making the slip of naming Jim Bannister. You never knew, even in this remote part of the mountains, who might have heard about that reward.

As for the woman, her fate if she should fall into the hands of the Cagles was none of Wes Dodd's concern. She was asking for anything that happened to her. . . .

Dewey Cagle said, "Just one problem. The lawman, here, is gonna have to have a bronc. He tried to promote one from old man Gillis, but got turned down."

"Did he, now?" Vern Cagle looked toward the barn. While they talked, Gillis and his helper had brought out a pair of fresh animals for the coach and, having backed them into place, were returning for more while the driver hitched up. Vern rubbed the ball of a thumb across his lean jaw. "Well," he said. "I reckon that old man knows better than to turn down a Cagle. I'll take care of this."

There was an interim then in which nothing happened. Over at the coach, the passengers were standing around waiting to load, but no one came from the barn with the rest of the team and the driver began to show his impatience; he paced back and forth beside his coach and once Dodd heard him exclaim testily, "What the hell are they doing?" Finally he cursed and started for the barn himself.

At that moment someone came out, but it wasn't Gillis or his helper. It was Vern Cagle, and he led a saddled horse. His cousin chortled at sight of him. "That ol' Vern boy!" he declared to Wes Dodd. "He don't take no guff from nobody!" And as his relative approached with the horse in tow: "How about it? Did he try to make a fuss?"

"He was a mite fretful to begin with," Vern conceded. "But he seen the light."

"What all you do to him?"

"Tell us later what you did to him," Wes Dodd interrupted curtly. "I want to get on with this."

"Why, sure," Vern Cagle said, and handed over the reins. "And look what else the man give me."

He held up an unlighted barn lantern, shook it so they could hear the slosh of kerosene. "Night tracking, it should come in handy."

In a moment all three were mounted. There was no saddle boot for the rifle and Dodd laid it across his lap, one hand holding it in place there. The horse Vern had promoted for him was a cold-jawed brute, a hammerheaded roan with scabs on its flanks from generous spurring. Probably it needed spurs, and Dodd had none. But he had the rifle, and when the animal tried to balk he let it have the stock, hard, a couple of times in the ribs. When it swung its head around with bared teeth, reaching for his leg, he kicked it in the jaw; after that it settled down and the three of them rode out of the yard.

As they passed the group of men still clustered about the stalled coach, someone yelled a question but received no answer. Then they'd left Ute Springs Station behind them.

Wes Dodd let the other two take the lead, still dubious as to what results he could expect from this pair of hillbillies. But it seemed likely they knew the country, and that was more than could be said for himself or, probably, for Bannister. If they thought they knew how to run a fugitive down for him, he felt he had no choice but to let them try.

They did seem in agreement. They didn't bother with the stage road but pushed straight on, for the black mass of timber at the foot of the mountain wall. Apparently there was a break in the trees, that he himself would have missed; they rode into this and the pines closed over them, letting in only a hint of light. Here they fell into a trail and took it single file, with Vern Cagle in the lead.

He pulled rein presently. "Pretty dark in here," he grunted. "Maybe weuns better have a go with that lantern, and see just what we're a-doing."

Dewey had taken charge of the barn lantern; he got it lit, and the circle of yellow light made odd, shifting patterns over the crowding timber as he swung down from the saddle. Wes Dodd could see now that they indeed were in a narrow trail, marked out by the repeated passage of horse traffic. He watched as Dewey walked about holding the lantern close to the ground, studying hoofmarks. He straightened finally with a shake of the head. "Nothin'," he told the other.

Vern, still mounted, pushed the hat back from his bony forehead. "We'll go on some," he decided. Dewey remounted, carrying the lighted lantern as they proceeded for perhaps another quarter of a mile. By now they were starting to climb, and Vern sent his cousin down again for another inspection.

Suddenly Dewey squatted on the heels of scuffed cowhide boots, for a closer look. He stabbed a pointing finger as he looked up in triumph. "Here it is! Here's *our* tracks, that we made comin' down—and the fresh sign on top. We got 'em ahead of us."

"Naturally," Vern said calmly.

Dodd couldn't hold back longer. "This trail isn't marked. What made you so sure they'd find it?"

"Hell! Weuns ain't exactly fools, mister," the other retorted, with a cold look. "We can figure out what happened here today—how you used the woman for bait, knowing he'd be meeting the stage, and you'd have your chance to nab him either here at Ute Springs, or somewheres else along the line.

"Anyway, it was only good sense he'd scout the place out some, before risking his hide. And to us that meant he'd likely have had this trail spotted, aforehand. And turns out, our thinkin' was correct. That satisfy you?"

Dodd nodded grudgingly. "I'm satisfied. Now, maybe you'll tell me where this trail leads. Looks to me that it heads straight over the mountain."

"You called 'er, mister." Dewey Cagle wagged his head and the barn lantern, sitting on the ground beside his squatting figure, cast his gaunt face into strange angles and hollows. "She leads right to Missouri Gulch."

"That's spelled M-i-s-e-r-y," his cousin put in dryly.

"To weuns, mister," Dewey continued, squinting up at the bounty hunter, "hit's home.

57

Been Cagles there for twenty year and longer. Only Cagles use this trail, for mule-packin' in grub and supplies—or, just ridin' down to Ute Springs for a change of grub and scenery, like me and Cousin Vern this evening. 'Tain't far, actually, but hit's a long way from most places."

"And the point is, mister," Vern Cagle added, with a coldly meaning stare, "you're gonna need us now, a helluva lot wuss than you thought five minutes ago! Cagles are clannish folk; leaving the Ozarks for Colorado ain't changed us any. Ain't nobody but kinfolk really welcome in the Gulch—and so you see, you're lucky having us along to vouch for you, and make things a mite easier once you get there."

Dewey agreed. "Hell, yes. Now, you take that other feller—the one you're chasing: *He* gets up there, won't take him long to find he's rid his tail into a hornet's nest. Him and his female, both."

And without a gun, and his hands shackled, Wes Dodd thought; if half of what they told him was really true, then Jim Bannister had done himself little good despite that damned trick with the scalding coffee, and his escape on the waiting horse. . . . Dodd suggested, "How do we know he won't leave the trail before he's got that far?"

"No danger of that—you'll see. Once you're on *this* trail, there's no gettin' off. Oh, no. He'll be ahead of us, all the way!"

"If you say so."

Dodd looked at his companions. They were uncouth and ignorant hillbillies, and it gave him no pleasure to deal with such men; but he saw no alternative, if they had told the truth about what he would find at the end of this poorly marked, seldom-traveled horse track. He said sourly, "I suppose I have to assume you know what you're talking about!"

"You sure as hell do, now don't you?" agreed Vern, with a wicked grin. And taking the reins, he told his cousin, "Time's a-wastin'. We won't be needin' the lantern no more. Get shut of it, and let's ride."

Dewey cranked up the lantern's chimney, blew out the flame. In its place, dim moonlight filtered through the trees, though the lantern's bright afterimage would linger for long minutes. There was a brief delay while Dewey hung the lantern by its bail, to a stub of pine branch where he probably meant to retrieve it at some convenient future time; then leather creaked and he was in the saddle.

With a growling word to his horse, Vern took the lead. Wes Dodd fell in behind Dewey Cagle and they went forward, the trail already climbing steeply through night-black timber.

CHAPTER V

For Jim Bannister, taking this trail up the mountain had been a last resort—better than letting himself be run to earth trying to escape along the open stage trace, better than finding a place to hole up and hide from a search party: With Stella's safety at stake, he simply couldn't afford to gamble.

His hope had been to gain time and cover some distance before the Cagles tumbled to the fact of his having found that trail, but now he was having misgivings. With the dun laboring under its double burden, he began to think a mountain goat must have laid out the erratic course they were being taken. There was simply no hope of making any time on it; and now, without warning, the timber fell away and left them high on the face of the rock wall—clinging to it like a fly on a windowpane, with the brilliant moonlight white and ghostly upon them.

As they moved ahead the tiring animal missed a step in loose rubble and started to slide back, raising a cloud of acrid rock dust. The animal snorted and regained footing, but Bannister heard Stella cry out, felt her hold about his waist tighten convulsively. He pulled in to let the dun settle; while it stood with lungs working like a bellows, he turned and looked at the woman's face that was pale as the moonlight, her eyes like dark stains.

"You all right?"

"If I can just manage to hang on!" She spoke lightly but he sensed the apprehension in the look she put below them, down the sheer fall of the mountainside toward black spires of timber far below.

"It's a better trail than it looks," Bannister assured her. "In spite of what the winters here do to it. Plainly it's seen quite a lot of traffic, and over a long period of time—pack trains, likely enough, as well as saddle animals. And the dun is surefooted. There's nothing to worry about."

As if to belie what he said, the animal shifted position and loose rock turned under one hoof. The horse gave a snort and tried to curvet in the narrow trail; more rock was dislodged and went spilling, a small landslide gathering behind it. The noise built and then died away again, sopped up by the lower timber.

Bannister could feel Stella trembling as she pressed herself against his back. He spoke sharply to the dun, knowing the horse was frightened and that, if it lost its head, it might very well back all three of them into empty space.

"Can't we get off this?" Stella asked in a voice that shook.

He pointed with both manacled hands. "I see

what looks like a cleft in the rock, yonder," he said. "Perhaps another hundred yards. We'll take it easy . . ."

A touch at the rein, a quiet word of encouragement, sent their mount forward, still uneasy and setting its hoofs warily. They left that particular danger spot, got onto firmer footing and soon were climbing again toward the black slot where the trail disappeared. The audible sound of the dun's breathing, and the bunching of its muscles, showed how hard it was working.

Then the opening, like a slit carved by a knifeblade, was just above them; they rode up into it, and the route abruptly leveled off. Night wind, that felt as though it came directly off some high snowfield, whistled eerily through the crevice. The dun's shoes raised clattering echoes off naked rock walls that rose above their heads, with the stars glittering far away.

Bannister heard Stella's sigh of relief. Over his shoulder he said, "We'll hope that was the worst of it . . ."

It did seem so. The fissure opened onto a fairly gentle slope strewn with boulders; here, the stars were like an explosion overhead and the moon shone frostily on the shoulders of peaks where unmelted ice still clung. The trail dropped into a long ravine, climbed out again onto the first of a series of benches that fell away, by gradual descent, until they were once more in timber. As they dismounted to stretch cramped muscles and let the dun have a breather, Stella pressed close to Bannister's side. They listened to the stillness of the chill mountain dark.

"What do you think?"

"I think I'm mostly curious," he told her. "Somebody went to a lot of work laying out this route. It has to lead somewhere." He knew the risks in going ahead, but if there were people then there was always a chance of getting rid of these handcuffs and, if he was lucky, even getting ahold of a gun. And that was essential: Bannister didn't dare tackle the perils of this wild high country as long as he was weaponless, with his hands shackled and Stella's safety dependent on him. He had no choice but to go on.

He aided her to remount and they rode on through the deepening night. As it grew steadily colder, Bannister became concerned for the woman—her traveling costume was never intended to keep her warm against the chill of the high peaks. If there had been any way to remove his own coat he would have insisted on her taking it, but of course that was impossible with steel bracelets locked on his wrists. Instead he halted long enough to get one of the blankets from his saddle roll; she put this around her shoulders and he saw how she huddled into its folds.

Short of stopping to make camp and build a

fire, there was nothing more he could think to do for her. And he felt beyond question that they should keep going.

"Listen!" Stella exclaimed suddenly. "I thought I heard a dog . . ."

Bannister had already reined in; the lonely baying came to them again, thin and lost in the quiet, carried on the night wind that breathed against their faces. Stella said, her voice hushed, "It is a dog, isn't it? Not a coyote, or a wolf."

"It's a hound," Bannister confirmed. "That full moon—it's got him bothered." He thought of the Cagles, suddenly. They were true hillbillies, judging from the talk and look of them. And that animal disturbing the night with its racket had the sound of a Missouri hunting dog.

He spoke to the weary dun. As they went ahead, the wind shifted; the sound of the dog faded.

In another minute Jim Bannister all but forgot him.

They had rounded a timbered shoulder, and here the land fell off with such dramatic suddenness that Bannister pulled up, sharply. Then he saw how the trail took a twist and dropped away down an easy grade. But he was in no hurry to go on, until he first studied what had opened before him.

This was the lower stretch of a deep, steep-walled depression, carved into the living granite of the mountains—known, in the parlance of gold-mining regions like this Colorado country, as a "gulch." The moon, about to drop its white face behind the westward peaks at his back, showed it extending a half mile or more from wall to wall at this point. There was timber, and here and there a gleam of silver water hinted at the creek that had carved this formation out of solid granite and now threaded the heart of it. The gulch lay visible for a distance in either direction, before darkness swallowed it. Obviously it headed up somewhere in the high peaks to the north. To the right, lower down, it seemed to play out into broken, impassable canyon country. He judged the hour as close to midnight.

The dun stood impassive, weary from carrying double over such a trail. Bannister absently patted the horse's shoulder as he considered; and Stella said, "It looks as though the trail goes down in there. Do you suppose this is where it ends?" And then, before he could answer: "You hear that? There's the dog, again!"

Bannister nodded without speaking. The lonesome bugling of the hound drifted clearly to them now from somewhere below; farther along the gulch another took up the cry and the two joined voices briefly in a mournful duet, as though aware that the moon was about to get away from them and slip from sight behind the mountains. After the first dog fell silent the other continued a moment longer, then abruptly broke off—perhaps its owner had tired of the racket and silenced it.

Scanning the darkness down there, Jim Bannister narrowed attention suddenly. He had picked out a square of yellow light. Even as he looked at it the light vanished; but he knew what he had seen was the gleam of a lamplit window that marked a house, or a cabin of some sort.

He lifted the reins. "Well," he said gruffly, "we might as well have a look at what we've got here . . ."

This trail chose the most convenient place for a drop into the gulch, but it was still an eerie experience in nearly total darkness. The dun took it gingerly, on braced forelegs; they seemed to descend forever as the lower trees came up to meet them. Then, abruptly, they were on level ground again.

It was a shade warmer than it had been where they were exposed to the sweep of wind, down off the snowfields of the peaks. Here by contrast the air was still, and the night so quiet Bannister could hear the distant voice of the creek. A horse track led northward through the pines. He turned into it, thinking it would lead in the general direction of that lighted window he'd seen. He went cautiously, probing the night with all his senses.

Then, just to his left and a little behind him, a voice spoke sharply: "Stand right where you're at!"

Bannister suppressed an oath, and downed an impulse to clap spurs to the dun—Stella, riding behind him, was the one who would be exposed to the danger of gunplay. He heard her draw a quick gasp of alarm. And as he halted the dun, two riders came out of the dense shadows.

For just an instant he had the irrational thought that they were Vern and Dewey Cagle, managed somehow to catch up, but he immediately decided that was hardly possible. While he waited the pair walked their horses forward, one swinging around the prisoners so as to close in from the other side. Bannister saw the gleam of a rifle barrel.

Holding the rifle steady across the swell of his saddle, the one who had spoken before gave a new command: "Put a light on yourself."

It would be impossible to obey without revealing that his hands were shackled, and Bannister decided he didn't want them to know that. Not moving, he answered shortly, "I couldn't if I wanted to. I haven't got a match."

That drew a grunt of displeasure, but the second man dug into his clothing and moments later a yellow spurt of flame sprung to life between his cupped hands. It seemed to flood the darkness; in the brief instant before it gutted out, Bannister had a look at his captors.

There could be no doubt about them being Cagles, even if the voice hadn't already revealed as much. Both had the family features—bony foreheads, hollow cheeks, faces that tapered to jutting, pointed jaws. He who held the rifle was an older man, with a grizzled mustache falling in horns to bracket his tight trap of a mouth; the other, who might have been his son, looked to be nearer the age of Dewey, or Vern. Piggish pale eyes studied the pair on the dun, and though they held no light of recognition that might indicate they knew who this tall, blond stranger was, Bannister had to clench his jaws as he endured their scrutiny.

He was glad when the match burnt down and flickered out, and the one who held it dropped it to the ground between their horses.

The older one demanded, "You ever seen 'em, Yance?"

"No, Pa," the younger answered promptly.

"Me either." The pale eyes seemed to burn in the darkness, studying the strangers by such of the moon's light as reached them here among the trees. "This place is kind of out of the way," the man told Bannister, his tone heavy with suspicion. "Suppose you tell us what you're doin' here."

Bannister had been busily groping for a plausible answer to that question; he gave the best he could invent on the spur of the moment. "I think we may be lost. My wife and I are trying to find a stage station. We were told there was

68

one somewhere hereabout. A place called Ute Mountain—something like that."

"Ute Springs?" Yance Cagle suggested.

"That must be it. We thought we were on the right trail, but we've been following it for hours and not seeming to get anywhere a stagecoach might figure to go!"

"Hell! You're only headed the wrong direction, is all!"

If Yance seemed inclined to accept the story, his father was clearly skeptical. "Just how'd you manage to get on this trail in the first place, mister? Where'd you start from?"

Bannister shook his head; he tried to sound completely bewildered. "Turned around the way I am, I don't think I can tell you. We were at a place called Mauger's Peak, this morning"— he supplied the name out of his rather sketchy knowledge of this region. "We've been out with a hunting party, after bighorns. In over a week, we never got a decent shot; finally my wife decided she'd had enough. We left the others and are trying to find a way out of the hills by ourselves."

"The both of you on one horse?" The question was sharply suspicious.

"We had an accident. Her animal threw her, and lamed itself." Bannister waited, having told his lie, and looking for the first indication whether it had been believed. At that moment the dun stretched its neck to sniff at Yance Cagle's horse; Bannister hauled it in, then caught his breath as the movement drew back the sleeves of his jacket for just a moment, revealing the glint of steel bracelets on his wrists. Right then, having these two see the handcuffs was the last thing he wanted.

And then his blood chilled at the sound of Yance Cagle's snickering laugh. "Hell! It couldn't be clearer, Pa. He's lying in his teeth!"

The older man swung his head; under the hatbrim's shadow his eyes peered at Yance. "Spell it out, boy."

One arm lifted, pointed at Bannister and then at the woman clinging behind his saddle. "I'll bet odds, if she's somebody's wife she ain't his'n! They're runnin' off together—*that's* what it amounts to! No wonder they've stuck to the back trails!"

The guess was an ingenious one, but it was so far off the truth that it caught Bannister by surprise. When he regained his tongue he decided that silence would look like guilt, and so he simply kept his mouth shut and watched Yance's father rub a hand across his face and down over his heavy mustache as he considered.

"What they're runnin' from," the older man said finally, "ain't any of my concern; but they've sure as hell run to the wrong place! Mister," he told the stranger, "if you want the stage station, you'll just have to turn around and follow this trail back the way you came."

Jim Bannister appeared to hesitate. He knew he still had to play his part convincingly if he hoped to keep them satisfied with their error. "It's been a hard day," he pointed out. "The lady's worn out. I don't suppose we could—?"

"No, you couldn't!" the elder Cagle told him flatly. "Us folks don't exactly cotton to outsiders—least of all, to havin' 'em bring their personal feuds in on top of us. So, if you-uns got a jealous husband tailing you, then you just take him somewheres else."

"I was thinking," Bannister ventured, not wanting to sound too easily persuaded, "maybe a fresh horse? This one's about used up."

"You heard!" Suddenly the rifle was lifted and pointed at the stranger's chest. "Now, don't force me to git unpleasant. Just turn that animal around."

"But—" He tried to get just the right note of despair into his voice. Then, as though resignedly giving up the argument, he gave the reins a jerk to back the dun and pull about. As they started away the man shouted after them, "And keep ridin'."

Bannister deliberately held to a slow walk, which wasn't difficult considering that the dun was really close to played out. There was the sound behind them of the two Cagles following, keeping pace and making sure they did as they were ordered; after a few minutes those sounds died. When he dared look back, Bannister could see neither rider in the scattered shadows under the trees. Apparently they were satisfied the threats had worked and these two people had been got rid of. Bannister felt the tension loosening from his muscles; he blew out his cheeks in relief.

Hearing a sound like a muffled sob from Stella, he halted the dun and turned to her. "Are you all right?" he demanded anxiously.

Only then did he realize she was laughing! "I never knew you could be such an accomplished liar!" Stella exclaimed, between gasps. "You had those two eating right out of your hand."

"A man never knows what he can do until he has to," Bannister admitted. "Though there was a bad moment when I was sure they'd seen the handcuffs!" He tried to speak lightly, but he felt a sudden pang of concern, listening to her; it occurred to him that her laughter held the sound of sheer exhaustion, that she was dangerously near to hysteria. He was just as pleased when she subsided.

The weariness and discouragement were plain to be heard as Stella asked, then, in a tiny voice, "Whatever are we going to do?—Those were relatives of the pair at the stage station, weren't they?"

"Absolutely. All from the same clan—we seem to have unearthed a hotbed of them. But it's no good to turn back and risk running into Wes Dodd . . . What about Yance and his father? Any sign of them now?"

She looked behind. "No. I don't think they're following us."

"That's good! How are you managing? Can you hang on just a little longer?"

"I—think so." She sounded game, but weary enough to drop.

"Afraid I'll have to ask you to try. And riding blind, the going's apt to be rough . . ."

Her arms came around his waist, holding her there. Jim Bannister spoke to the tired horse and sent it up a knoll, and once again into the timber.

CHAPTER VI

Sometime in the next half hour, as they rode northward through the gulch, the moon finally dipped behind the peaks and then real darkness settled. With the dun feeling its way, virtually step by cautious step among these close-growing trees, there was no hope of making any time. Presently the horse seemed to drop into a game trail of sorts and followed that for a distance, with only such starlight as shook down through the branches to show Bannister where he was riding.

Stella clung to her place, uncomplaining, but Bannister knew she was going on sheer willpower. He was weary enough himself, and as he thought of what she was undergoing for love of him, a deep respect and devotion welled up inside Jim Bannister. Once or twice he tried to summon up words of encouragement, but they sounded hollow enough. They were both in a bad spot and they simply had to tough it out.

Then, abruptly, the trees opened at the foot of a brushy slope. Below them was cleared land, and a cluster of buildings. Bannister thought the house could be the same one he had noticed from up on the rim of the gulch. It was a low, log structure; there was no lamplight showing now in the black openings of its windows, and the scatter of sheds behind it were likewise dark and silent in the heart of the night.

Satisfied with a first cautious survey, he said aloud, "This will do."

He stepped down and, awkwardly because of his manacled wrists, helped Stella to alight. When her feet touched the ground, her knees buckled with weariness and Bannister had to grip an arm to steady her. She rested her head against him for a moment, then gathered her strength and stepped back; he saw her lift a hand uncertainly and pass it through the wind-tangled mass of her hair.

"What—what is it?"

He explained. "Somehow or other I've got to get these things off my wrists. That place down there looks asleep; maybe I can locate a file in one of the sheds. Perhaps, with any luck, something to use for a weapon."

He heard her quick intake of breath. "Oh—be careful!"

"I've lasted this long by being careful," Bannister pointed out. "You stay put—don't move from this spot; I want to be sure of finding you. Be ready to quiet the horse if he should start acting up."

"Of course."

She was plainly reluctant to let him take the risk. Bannister touched her shoulder in reassurance, and then turned to make his way down the slope toward the quiet cabin below.

In moonless darkness, it was treacherous footing, and his shackled wrists hampered him in keeping his balance. Once a bullbat swooped past his head, so startlingly close that he missed a step and nearly went down; he paused a moment to recover his bearings.

Then he was at the foot of the slope, and the faint gleam of wire around a patch of root crops lay before him, with the buildings just beyond. He saw a pole corral with a single horse in it. There appeared to be no barn or any structure, other than the cabin itself, that was larger than a shed. The cabin, of peeled logs, bulked darkly to his right; he avoided it, aiming the other way.

One of these smaller buildings, he hoped, would turn out to be a toolshed—the likeliest place to find something that would help him remove these damned steel bracelets. While he looked, he had to take his chances that whoever might be in the house was a sound sleeper.

Within the first of the outbuildings, as he cautiously approached, he heard a faint contented clucking and stirring and caught the distinct odor of poultry; he passed that one by. A few yards farther on was a small square structure with a simple wooden catch on the door. When he opened the door it emitted a squeal of unoiled hinges that made him freeze where he stood, a faint sweat breaking out on him. But the noise could hardly have been as loud as it sounded to his own ears, for though he waited, there was no reaction from yonder at the house. Bannister eased out a breath, and stepped inside.

It was pitch dark; his groping hands searched and found nothing more than a number of gunnysacks ranged upon the floor. Seed, he thought or feed for the chickens—the floor was gritty with it. Quickly certain that there was nothing of any use to him here, he withdrew, tempted to leave the door open rather than risk that squeaking hinge. Still, it wouldn't be fair to the man who owned those bags of grain. Bannister had nothing against him, and so he managed to get the door pushed shut with a minimum of noise, and fastened.

He looked around, debating. Everything was still quiet; the horse in the corral stood droop-headed and probably asleep. So far, so good.

One structure, set off by itself, was obviously a privy; that left a couple more to be checked out. If he failed to find what he wanted there, he had better be going—he was already stretching his luck. Besides, he could imagine the anxiety Stella was enduring, waiting for him up there on the hill.

Moving on across an open space, Bannister caught an empty tin can with his boot toe and sent it clattering. This yard seemed to be littered with trash; he watched his step more carefully until he attained the blind side of a low, slant-roofed structure whose use he didn't immediately identify. He went forward, hunting a door.

Instead, he discovered a stout pen built against the forward end, five feet high and fashioned of horizontal jackpine poles. And as he paused beside it, there was a rush of padded feet and something smashed into the poles with a lunge that shook them from top to bottom. Startled, Bannister leaped away from the fence—and the night split apart as two flat, menacing heads reached through the bars for him, all snarling fangs and raucous baying.

Bannister swore. Above the clamor of the raging hounds, there was an angry roar now from inside the house. He had barely got back into the shadows against the shed wall when a man came bursting out, shouting and cursing at the sudden racket.

He was barefoot, in long johns that made a dim blur as he advanced across the yard. Bannister saw him stoop; when he came up, each hand held a length of stovewood. His first throw was wild, and the wood struck the shed only a foot from Bannister and made him cringe as it bounced off, just missing his crouching form. The second time, the man's aim was truer and the missile, spinning end for end, arced neatly above the dog-run fence. Bannister heard the thump as it struck living flesh and bone, and the baying of one of the animals broke off in yelps of injury.

"Gawddam dogs!" their owner bawled at them. "Spoon! You, Annie! *Shet up!*" They subsided, and Bannister thought he heard them slink back into the openface shed, out of range. Stillness settled again, as the man stood out there in the middle of the yard in his underwear, muttering and cursing to himself. Jim Bannister stayed where he was, half expecting at any moment to be discovered.

At that instant, he became aware of horses arriving in the night, and he knew it was too late to make a move when, abruptly, three riders came cantering into the yard. The owner of the dogs turned as Vern Cagle sang out, "Hello! That you, Cousin Heck?"

"Vern?" The newcomers pulled up; the man continued, "You-uns is ridin' a little late, hain't you? Who's that you got there?"

"Dewey," the other answered. "And a stranger."

"A stranger—in the gulch?"

"That's right, Heck. Feller we met down to Ute Springs . . . Mr. Dodd, this here's our cousin, Heck Cagle."

"Lemme fetch the lantern," Heck grunted suspiciously, and made off toward the house without giving the newcomer a chance to speak. While they were waiting, the three came down from their saddles with the obvious stiffness of long hours of riding. Only a few yards from where they stood, Bannister tried to make himself even less visible in the shadows piled against the shed. Thought of a lighted lantern had started him sweating a little.

Inside the house, a match flickered to life; a wick took flame and its glow steadied as the chimney was lowered into place. Now Heck returned, padding on bare feet and holding the lantern high. The swaying light reached dangerously close to Bannister's crouching figure.

It revealed the dog-owner's face, gaunt and black-bearded to the eyes, as he studied the stranger his kin had brought with them. Dewey Cagle spoke up. "Mr. Dodd's a Pinkerton man, Heck. He's on a trail, and we're lending him a hand."

Pinkerton man! Well, Bannister thought, it was probably as good a story as any they might have concocted. Vern and Dewey understood their people. They would know if these Cagles were more apt to suffer the presence of an agency detective than of someone who was supposed to be a lawman encroaching on their territory.

Wes Dodd endured the scrutiny by lanternlight calmly enough. He told Heck, "I'd appreciate knowing if you've seen any other strangers tonight, besides myself."

"Outsiders are let to know we don't care for

'em here in Missouri Gulch, mister," Heck Cagle told him firmly. "And if there's more than you, then they sure hain't been near *my* place."

"They're around somewheres," Vern said. "We've had 'em ahead of us, all the way from Ute Springs. Mr. Dodd's been hired by the railroad to run 'em down, and he's payin' us to help."

"Railroad stickups, huh? What would these fellers look like, Vern?"

"One's a woman, actually, and when last seen the man was wearing a pair of handcuffs. Besides that, they got just one hoss, between 'em. So, it ain't too likely you'd miss 'em."

"Sure as hell ain't!" the other grunted. "Not from a description like that."

"Well, there's fifty dollars in it for Vern and me if we catch up with 'em," Dewey said. "You keep an eye out. Meanwhile we aim to be alertin' everybody in the gulch . . ."

Bannister had suddenly heard enough. It occurred to him that the lanternlight in their eyes would have these men temporarily blinded; risky as it was, this could be the one best moment he was going to have for sneaking away from here. On that thought he got his feet under him, straightened with painful caution. When no one's eyes were drawn in his direction, he tried a stealthy step toward the rear corner of the shed.

But the dogs, even though quelled by their master, were still well aware of Bannister. He had heard them, just inches away, snuffling at chinks in the siding and whimpering a little over the unfamiliar scent. Now his movements stirred them again. All at once blunt claws were tearing the logs, the whimperings turned to snarls and yelps of frenzy as they tried to get through at him.

In a crouch, Bannister froze as the heads of the men yonder swung about. Dewey Cagle demanded, "What's itching them fool dogs of yourn, Heck?"

"Damned if I know," their owner grunted. "They brought me out, only minutes before you-uns showed up. A varmint after my chickens, maybe."

"The birds sound peaceful," Vern Cagle pointed out. And then from Dewey: "Hey! You don't reckon—?"

Heck swore, and suddenly he was heading for the dog shed, bringing the lantern with him. Bannister waited no longer. He lunged up and took off at a run.

That raised a startled yell—they all saw him, of course. Just as he reached the shed corner someone—he would bet it was Dodd—got his rifle up and threw off a shot. Its report broke the night apart; muzzle flash seemed almost to light up the whole yard as a bullet struck the log siding, missing him only by inches. Then he had put the corner of the shed between and when a second gun joined in, it shot at nothing.

Time for stealth was over; Bannister ran openly, long legs eating the distance across the dark yard. He stumbled once but caught his footing and went on, expecting at every moment to hear boots pounding after him. Pursuit seemed to be delayed, for some reason. He had reached the feed shed and hauled up there a moment to catch his breath, when over the racket of the dogs he caught the first sound of hoofbeats, and understood: He might have guessed that, rather than come after him on foot, Dodd and Vern and Dewey would take the time to catch up their waiting horses.

Not hesitating, Bannister fumbled at the wooden catch and cracked the shed door open, just wide enough for him to slip through. There was no way to fasten it from the inside so he gripped the edge to hold it in place, with a spare inch of gap between the panel and its frame. Standing in that musty darkness, surrounded by sacks of grain, he was well aware that he might have put himself in a trap; but it was the best he could do.

Already the horsemen were pounding up, and he held his breath as they reined in and he heard them milling around within yards of his hiding place. They were yelling questions back and forth, laced with profanity and excitement.

Suddenly a nasal Cagle voice shouted, "Hey!

I think I see him yonder!" In an instant they all were gone again, in what they obviously thought was pursuit of the fugitive.

Bannister slipped quickly out of hiding, taking long enough to fasten the door catch. He was wondering about the man named Heck—there wouldn't have been time for him to get mounted, even if he wanted to join the hunt. He might have gone back to the house, perhaps to get some clothes on. The frenzied dogs, meanwhile, seemed almost out of their minds, and even the chickens in their nearby shed had been roused by all the excitement and were squawking and making a commotion. But for the moment Jim Bannister was alone and free, while up on the slope he could hear those riders quartering about, calling back and forth, hunting him.

And then he remembered Stella, waiting, and he groaned at the thought of them blundering across her by accident. Because he couldn't stand there and let that happen, Bannister turned his face to the slope and started running.

He placed the noise of searching riders somewhere to his right, as he made as directly as possible for the black edge of timber. It seemed impossible to make any distance. He kept missing his footing on the uneven ground, crashing through brush he couldn't see, making noise he felt sure must tell his enemies exactly where he was. At last he had to pause for breath and to get his bearings—and as he did, hoofbeats shook the ground and the dark bulk of a horse and rider suddenly appeared as from nowhere, coming straight toward him.

The animal tossed its head as a hand pulled in the reins. Stella Harbord spoke from the dun's back, her voice tight with excitement. "Jim! Jim, is that you?"

Concern for her made the exclamation burst from him: "You shouldn't be out here! I told you—!" There was no time for more, for just then a shout went up and he knew they had been sighted. He swore, and lunged for the horse.

Stella didn't need to be told what to do. She vacated a stirrup for him, caught his arm to steady him as he swung up behind her, and then ducked her head so that he could pass his manacled arms down to encircle her and take the reins from her hands. A quick glance showed, dimly, the figures of three horsemen converging toward them across the open slope. Turning back, he settled himself as well as he could on his uncertain perch behind the saddle, and kicked the dun hard.

It lunged forward, all but unseating him. Yonder, someone gave a yell and a gun went off; the crack of the report sounded thinly, but the bullet came nowhere near.

Then the dun was leaping for the nearest timber. A few lunging strides, and blackness swallowed them up.

CHAPTER VII

The instant they were into the trees, they had to halt their pell-mell rush and let the horse more or less pick its own way. Despite the chill of the night Bannister sweat a little over the slowdown, but it helped to remember that his enemies, too, were going to have just as hard a time making any speed through this close-standing timber, in the dark.

The dun had had a short quarter hour of rest, which should help. Still, it had been hard pressed tonight and it couldn't go on forever. Sooner or later it would play out. He didn't let himself think about what would happen then.

Listening for sounds of pursuit, he heard instead Stella's anxious voice as she turned to stammer a question, across her shoulder: "What was all the shooting? I heard it and almost died!"

"I ran into some bad luck," he grunted. "It's Dodd and the Cagles who are after us—he's hired them at fifty dollars apiece to help run me down. That time they almost earned their money!"

There was no more talking; she seemed to know that it took all Bannister's attention to keep the horse moving through the jackpine, guiding it as best he could. Once, behind them, they heard a voice shout something and another faintly answer. Except for that they might almost have thought they were alone, with no one pressuring them.

Nevertheless they were being herded steadily northward along the wall of the gulch, the going becoming steeper and tougher with every minute. There came a time when Bannister felt he must manage somehow to locate a way down to level ground, but when he tried it he found himself at the edge of a fault slip, a sheer drop of fifty feet or more. So that route was closed; as he headed again into the trees, he had a sudden feeling that now, if never before, they were in real trouble.

There just might not be any way out of this.

He didn't mention his concern to Stella. Instead, he tightened his arms around her and said in her ear, "Sit tight. The going may get rough . . ." To turn back would mean riding straight into the hands of those men who were hunting them. He could only keep the dun forging ahead and fighting the worsening terrain. And now, abruptly, he came out upon a place where every stick of timber disappeared, shaved off the face of the cliff at some time or other by the fall of an avalanche. Reining up, he heard Stella's gasp of dismay. She knew as well as he that they were stopped.

Ahead was nothing; somewhere behind them were their enemies. But when he raised his head, starlight showed a possible escape: It looked from here as though erosion had been at work, carving the steep higher reaches of the cliff into a mounting series of rock ledges that were dotted with stunted trees and scrub.

Bannister took a long breath. "Well," he said, "looks like this is where we get down. Here—take the reins for a minute." As she kept the horse steady he slipped from his place and then reached up to help her dismount. Stella obeyed without question, but her movements were slow and heavy with weariness. She watched him in silence as he hooked the dun's reins on the saddlehorn and then pointed the horse in the direction they had come.

He nearly faltered, then, at the actual fact of abandoning the horse and setting themselves afoot. But he didn't have any other answer. He brought the palms of both manacled hands down sharply against the animal's haunch. The dun tossed its head, and plunged away.

For just a moment he stood listening to it crashing through scrub growth; then the rising wind covered all other sounds. He turned to Stella and seized her arm.

"That ought to give them something to confuse them," he said. "A few minutes at least. I only hope they don't shoot him!" He added, "Now, it looks like we climb. Think you're up to it?"

"I can try."

She answered gamely enough. He squeezed her

arm in reassurance, saying gruffly, "Follow me," and moved to take the lead.

It was a scramble. The wall of the gulch was nearly perpendicular here. They had to mount from ledge to ledge, following each one as far as it would take them and then finding a way to climb through clawing brush and shifting rubble to the next one above it. Night wind, whistling among the rock crannies, was a frigid punishment when it hit bodies that were already drenched with sweat.

The one satisfaction was in knowing their enemies would never be able to follow them here on horseback. Bannister began to feel that with this maneuver they'd lost Dodd and the Cagles, at least for the time being.

Stella worried him, though. He was having trouble enough himself and he could imagine what it was costing her, even if she had never once complained. He could hear her nearly sobbing with exertion, and when he turned to give her a hand up a tough stretch he could tell from her trembling just how close she was to playing out. This, after a tiring stagecoach journey, and the long horseback ride up from Ute Springs with all its tensions and discomfort, was enough to drain anyone's strength.

Suddenly he made his decision. Turning to the woman he said, "This is far enough. I don't see any use in going till we drop. There's a place right here we can hole up and make ourselves comfortable, after a fashion—for a few hours at least."

It touched him to see how she swayed in utter weariness. "I won't quarrel with that!" Stella assured him in a shaking voice. "I was awfully close to saying I was sorry, but I just couldn't take another step. . . ."

"No reason to be sorry," Bannister told her. "You've done wonders. You never cease to amaze me!"

It wasn't a cave Bannister had found—actually, little more than a narrow crack where softer rock between resistant layers had eroded away, leaving a space just wide enough to crawl into. As they lay stretched out there, the wind could not reach them and the rock beneath them retained some of the heat from the day. Side by side, they listened to the stillness and talked quietly, for the comfort and companionship of their own voices.

"Who *are* these people?" Stella asked. "Do you have any idea at all?"

"The Cagles? Well, it's plain enough they're all one clan. Transplanted to Colorado from the Ozark hills, would be my guess—I heard one of them say they called this place 'Missouri Gulch.' And I think they must have been here quite some time."

"But why? Why do they stay? Out here in the middle of nowhere . . ."

"It's the kind of life they would always have been used to," he pointed out. "As you know, 'gulch' is a mining country term. Maybe they originally came looking for gold."

"The whole clan of them?"

"Why not? These people stay together," Bannister added. "One thing we do know— they're suspicious of outsiders; the pair we ran into on the trail proved that. And it took Vern and Dewey, both, to persuade the fellow at the cabin it was all right to let Wes Dodd on the place."

Stella was silent a long time. Finally she said, "You don't sound as though there's much hope of finding anyone who might help us . . ."

"No hope at all, I'm afraid. Dodd has got Vern and Dewey on his side, with his offer of fifty dollars apiece; and they'll see to it the others go along. For that price they'll turn the place inside out, hunting for us."

"Then we haven't a chance!"

"We'll have to make our own chances," Bannister said bleakly.

He shifted position, trying to get more comfortable, and the handcuffs scraped against stone. She laid a hand on his wrist. "I was just wondering," she said. "Is there any way to break those things off? With a rock, perhaps?"

"Dodd would have the best," he answered. "These are the hardest steel—no rock would make a dent in them." He flexed his wrists gingerly and winced; he was glad for the darkness so Stella could not see how they were chafing his flesh, almost unbearably. Changing the subject he said, "It's going to be morning in a few hours. Maybe, when we can get a look at this country by daylight, something will suggest itself. Right now we better get some rest while we have the opportunity."

Stella murmured something that sounded like weary agreement. Somewhere in their flight, the blanket had been torn from her shoulders; feeling her press against him for warmth, he turned his head and received her kiss. Soon afterward Bannister heard the slow and steady sound of her breathing and knew she was asleep.

Great tenderness came over him—he could only guess at the depth of her weariness. He was tired enough himself, but the predicament they were in weighed on him so that he found himself staring into the darkness, traveling the futile treadmill of his own speculations as the night grew older around them.

At the search that seemed to produce no results, Wes Dodd was beginning to burn with a cold fury; now he vented it in savage sarcasm, against the two who were supposed to be helping him. As his tongue grew sharper, Dewey Cagle lost his own temper and began to scream rebuttals in a voice that rose higher, tone by tone; the older Vern Cagle for his part simply refused to answer to anything, which only helped to make Dodd seethe.

Having chased the frightened dun through nearly half a mile of brush and timber before discovering that the animal carried an empty saddle, they knew now that the fugitives were afoot. They let the animal go and turned back to try and pick up the trail, but an hour later they were still hopelessly floundering. And Wes Dodd could no longer contain himself.

With scathing bitterness he reminded his companions, "You're supposed to be the ones who know this country like their hip pockets. I could have done this well on my own, and I've never seen the place before—and neither had the man who's making fools of you both!"

"Nobody hain't been made fools of, mister!" Dewey Cagle retorted angrily. "Hit's moon dark, damn it! Cain't see your own hand in front of you—so, how you expect anyone to pick up a trail?"

"By daylight they'll be gone for good."

"Hain't likely," Dewey insisted. "Not if we stay 'twixt them and the trail they followed in here. We'll bottle 'em up, and sooner or later run 'em to ground."

Dodd considered that, in skeptical silence. The three sat their horses, the tired animals sagging under them, the wind pushing against them and filling the night with deceptive sound. Vern Cagle, opting to stay out of the argument, said nothing; his kinsman and the manhunter glared at each other, dimly visible shapes in the blackness.

Wes Dodd said suddenly, "Those dogs! Are they good for anything?"

"What dogs?" Dewey countered. "You mean, Cousin Heck's Spoon and Annie?"

"I mean those two hounds down in that pen, damn it!" Dodd answered on short temper. "I don't happen to be acquainted with them by name. But I take it they've got noses—and they shouldn't need daylight to track down a scent."

The younger man sounded dubious. "Heck uses them on cat, and bear, and other varmints. He ain't never run a man with 'em."

"Well, there's a first time for everything; so— go get them. If you expect to be paid," Dodd added heavy warning, "you'd better stop arguing with me and do something to earn it."

And as Dewey hesitated, Vern shifted position with a popping of saddle leather and said gruffly, "Go ahead, Dewey. The man knows what he wants. Tell Heck to come up, and bring his animals . . ."

With no further word of argument, Dewey Cagle reined away on his mission.

This meant a time of waiting. Dodd got down, carrying Bannister's rifle, and paced restlessly up and down—busy with his thoughts, the glow of a lighted cigar faintly touching the hard planes of his face as he drew deeply on it. Vern Cagle, for his part, hitched over to a comfortable position in the saddle, hooked a knee around the pommel and lapsed into immobility; he might almost seem to have fallen asleep that way, except for his pale stare that followed the figure of the manhunter, passing and returning under the swaying trees.

Neither spoke a word, in a long half hour.

Then, abruptly, riders were approaching. Dewey Cagle's voice sounded, shouting his cousin's name; the latter straightened and lowered his boot into the stirrup and called an answer, and the new arrivals homed in on it. As they rode up, their horses made considerable racket shouldering through the brush.

Heck Cagle had Spoon and Annie on the saddle with him, a way of traveling they were seemingly accustomed to on the way to taking up a chase. Heck appeared to be in a growling mood and Dewey explained, "He'd already gone back to bed. Wouldn't hardly come at all, 'thout I threatened him."

"This is just plain damned foolishness!" the dogs' owner declared tartly. "A night as black as this, we'll break our own necks and the dogs', too!"

But Wes Dodd merely took the cigar from his lips long enough to say two words: "Fifty dollars." That settled it. Heck still grumbled but, no longer arguing, he dumped the dogs unceremoniously off his lap and then stepped down to join them. They leaped soundlessly about his legs, plainly eager for the chase.

"All right. Whereabouts did you-uns lose the sign?" he demanded.

"If we knew that," Dodd reminded him tartly, "would we be asking you to find it for us?"

"Near as we can figure," Vern Cagle added, "about here is where they went and give us the slip. Dewey likely told you they're afoot. But if'n the dogs don't pick up sign on them, hain't nuthin' more can be done, short of daylight."

With that much to go on, Heck went through a brief ceremony, kneeling before each of his dogs in turn and talking to them quietly, explaining the problem, while they went nearly frantic with whining, tail-wagging eagerness. Straightening finally, he slipped the rawhide leashes and with a clap of his hands shouted, "Go, dogs!" And they went.

It was a confused operation. The men, waiting, listened to the hounds coursing about in the brush, snuffling and whining in their throats, eager to pick up some kind of scent. Suddenly one began a frantic baying and started away with Heck running after it, only to return minutes later swearing and cuffing the animal ahead of him. "Spoon treed him a damn squirrel!" he grunted in answer to Dewey's excited question. "Now, will you git to it, you dogs? We ain't got all night!"

"All night is what it appears likely to take," Wes Dodd observed sourly.

The performance continued, with the Cagles yelling suggestions and Heck growing steadily angrier at his animals. Dodd said nothing at all, he merely watched and worked on his cigar. At last he took what was left of his cigar from his mouth, looked at the glowing end, dropped it and ground it out under a heel. "This is getting nowhere," he decided. "We'll give it up till morning."

Heck called his hounds in and they came, crestfallen and whining their apologies. "They jist don't know what they're lookin' for, or where to start," he explained in their defense. "Had you a garment or something, that would give 'em the scent . . ."

"Forget it. *And* the dogs." Wes Dodd swung onto his horse's back and reined away without waiting for an answer. Vern and Dewey looked at each other and followed more slowly, leaving Heck to leash his dogs and ride after them in defeat.

It appeared to be accepted that they would stay at Heck Cagle's for the night, and resume the hunt by daylight. When they rode into the yard, Dodd dismounted and left his horse for someone else to see to. To Heck he said, "If you haven't already, you had better check around and see if anything's missing. It would be my guess he was looking for a way to get those shackles off. A rasp, something of that sort."

Heck merely grunted and rode off toward the dog shed. His cousins left their horses on trailing reins and followed Dodd into the cabin.

A lamp had been left burning on the crude homemade table; Vern turned up the wick and Dodd took the place in at a glance. Heck appeared to live alone. His home was primitive enough—a rock-and-daub fireplace for cooking and heat, furniture that had been obviously knocked together on the spot, a pole bunk in one corner. Aside from a few cheap cooking utensils, and some rusty traps hanging on the wall, there wasn't much else that would have to have been packed in from outside, over that tortuous trail.

Wes Dodd dropped his hat on the table, pulled out a rawhide-bottomed chair and slacked into it. "Anything around here to drink?" he demanded irritably.

"Why, sho." As though he knew just where to look, Vern Cagle went to the unmade bunk and hauled out a jug from underneath. "We make this ourselves," he explained as he brought it back to the table. "Nothin' like corn, on a night with a nip to it." He drew the cork with strong white teeth, and poured into a tin cup he picked up somewhere. Setting it in front of the guest, he said pleasantly, "Here you air. Drink up." And he proceeded to do as much himself, but instead of using a cup he simply tilted the jug across an elbow and drank directly from it.

Dodd picked up the cup. He took a dubious swallow, made a face. "That is the most abominable stuff I ever tasted!"

"Hit *is* good, hain't it?" Dewey Cagle agreed, as he took the jug from his cousin and helped himself. Wes Dodd shuddered a little and set the rest of his drink on the table unfinished.

Wiping a sleeve across his lips, Vern eased into a chair opposite. "Now, don't you be fretful about that feller we're after, Mr. Dodd," he said reassuringly. "Him and his woman found 'em a hidey-hole, most like; but come daylight, we'll turn this gulch inside out and we'll find 'em. Nothin' to worry about."

Not convinced, Wes Dodd took the occasion to remind him, "If we *don't* find them, you neither of you get a penny. I hope you understand that."

"Well, now . . ." Vern Cagle's pale eyes seemed to change color slightly, in the gleam of the oil lamp. "There's just one little thing about that I'd like to straighten out." He lifted his stare above the other man's head. "Dewey!" he said suddenly.

It was a signal. Dodd had, for the moment, lost track of the younger cousin. Belatedly he started up, right hand moving toward the gap in his coat;

in that same instant he was seized from behind, forced back into the chair with both arms trapped. Taken by surprise, he fought to free himself. The table screeched on the floorboards as a flailing boot struck it. But there was surprising strength in the arms that held him pinned.

"Hold him steady," Vern warned his cousin; and then to the prisoner, grinning a little, "And you just sit peaceful, Mr. Dodd. Weuns don't figure to hurt you none, if you don't do nothin' to make us."

Rage exploded from the manhunter. "What do you think you're up to?"

"Just checkin' out something." Vern reached across the table and lifted Dodd's sixshooter from the spring holster under his coat, laid it aside. That done, he probed again and this time, in an inner pocket, located a packet of folded papers. He gave a grunt of satisfaction as he brought it out—it could have been what he was looking for.

Dodd warned him, half choking on his anger, "Those are my personal possessions!"

"Yeah." Not in the least disturbed, Vern Cagle wet a dirty thumb and, unfolding the papers, began separating and laying them out on the table before him, like a man dealing playing cards. They proved to be reward notices, each with a man's picture and bold lettering specifying descriptions and charges and the head money to be earned by capture and delivery. When he came to one in particular, Vern's hands went still. He laid the rest aside, then, no longer interested in them. He stared at the one he held until his cousin asked impatiently, "Well? What do hit say, Cousin Vern?"

The pale eyes lifted to Wes Dodd, still held helpless in Dewey's grasp. Face stern, Vern Cagle said, "This lawman has been lying to us. Hain't no fifty-dollar train robber we're lookin' for. Take a look!" And he held up the reward notice and turned it for Dewey to see.

The latter squinted at it studiously. "What's all them zeros come to, Cousin Vern?"

Vern told him and his eyes rounded. "Twelve—thousand—dollars! They *ain't* that much money!"

"If they is," the other promised coldly while his pale stare skewered the man in the chair opposite, "then weuns is gonna git our share of it. Right, Mr. Dodd?"

The manhunter, struggling with emotion, found his voice. "Let me loose, damn you!"

"Soon as a few things is got straight," Vern told him calmly. "First off, our deal still holds: Since our kinfolks don't cotton to outside lawmen stickin' their noses into our affairs, we won't say nothin' about you bein' one. 'Course, I don't really think you air," he added, showing his teeth in a hard grin. "With all these reward notices in your pocket, I figure you, now, for nothin' but a damn bounty hunter—right?"

Dodd merely ground his jaws, so that the muscles at the base of them bunched hard; but he said nothing. Vern continued.

"Second: Weuns go right ahead, like was promised, helpin' you catch this—" he glanced at the paper to make sure of the name "—this Jim Bannister feller; and we guarantee our kin will help. But they ain't to know just who we're really after, or the price on him. 'Cause if they did, some I know would likely want cut in.

"Me and Dewey, though, we hain't greedy. I reckon weuns can be right satisfied, between us, to settle for no more'n half."

"Half!"

"Six thousand for us, the same for you," Vern continued blandly. "And I don't know whut that is if it hain't downright generous—when you consider, except for us, you don't stand a prayer of layin' eyes on so much as a penny of it. You're a smart man, Mr. Dodd," he admonished, wagging a finger. "You ought to see that for yourself. You *do* see it?" he prodded, when he got no answer.

Into the crackling tension, a new sound intruded—bootsteps, approaching the cabin door. Dewey Cagle warned sharply, "Cousin Heck's coming. You better talk fast!"

The pale eyes probed at the prisoner. "A deal, Mr. Dodd? or—do you want me to show him this paper?"

Wes Dodd swore. "A deal!" he snapped hoarsely.

At once, Vern Cagle showed his teeth in a grin. "Leave him go, Dewey," he ordered pleasantly. And as Dodd jerked free of the grip that held him pinned, Vern pushed the papers, and the sixshooter, across the table; they were snatched up and vanished into the manhunter's clothing, before the door creaked open on its leather hinges.

Heck Cagle, entering with the lantern he had just extinguished, told them, "Blamed if I could see anything missin' from the toolshed—anything a feller could use to bust a pair of handcuffs . . ."

"Fine—fine," Vern said. But it was doubtful if anyone had really paid him much attention.

CHAPTER VIII

The night seemed interminable.

Even protected as they were in their niche, the mountain chill reached Bannister and the woman as stored warmth leaked out of the rocks. The wind rose, and seemed to search them out. A black roof of clouds moved across the stars, and toward morning an icy rain began; the wind flung it at them like glancing needles that they could not escape. They pressed close together and Bannister shielded Stella's body with his own as best he could, feeling the long shudders that ran uncontrollably through her as the cold took over. Finally, exhausted, they both slept.

By daylight the storm was over; the clouds broke apart and let sunlight shaft through, to raise streamers of mist from the wet rock faces and, slowly, lift the temperature. Bannister had wakened early and, letting Stella sleep, left their hiding place to walk the stiffness out of his joints and soak up the sun's welcome warmth, while he surveyed the land below them as morning light began to infiltrate the shadows of the gulch.

He found himself thinking again about the sounds that had reached them last night, an hour or more after going into their hole: they had been, unmistakably, the voices of hounds searching out a trail, and they'd sounded uncomfortably near.

Bannister had listened in some apprehension before the baying and yelping had finally ceased, very much as though the dogs had been called off. Well, one thing good about that storm—it would have washed out any tracks. If his enemies were really using Heck's animals to pick up his scent, there was little chance that they'd have any better luck now, trying it again by daylight. . . .

When Stella crawled from their niche and came to join him, Bannister was standing motionless, staring at the barren lift of rocky rim on the opposite side of the gulch; he turned as she spoke. He thought she looked wan and drained, but she managed a smile for him as he asked, anxiously, "How are you?"

"Fine—I think!" she said in a rueful tone. "After a night like that, it's hard to tell. That sun does feel good, though . . ." She lifted her head to welcome its touch, filling her lungs with the thin and bracing air of morning.

But a moment later her expression changed and her brown eyes widened. "Oh!" she exclaimed. He realized she had caught sight of his wrists, for the first time seeing they were raw and swollen from the chafing of the manacles.

Bannister looked down at them, and moved his shoulders in a shrug. "Nothing to be done about it. Or about breakfast, I'm afraid," he added, to change the subject. "At least, I don't notice anything that looks edible."

She let a slight smile touch her lips. "Do you hear me complaining?" She spoke quietly, but her comment confirmed what he already knew—that she was game to the core.

She placed her hands at the small of her back and pushed against them, stretching cramped muscles, and after that began doing something about the tangle of her hair. Bannister watched—her arms raised, her head a little bent so he could see the green glint from one of a pair of earrings he had given her. He felt a certain male wonderment for the swift and dextrous movements with which she took down her wealth of brown hair, shook it out and set about fashioning it into a single wide braid.

Around the pins in her mouth, she asked, "Have you decided what happens next?"

"I've got an idea of sorts. Only wish I had my field glasses for about five minutes."

They would have made an extra, unmanageable burden, and he'd reluctantly left them on his saddle when he turned the dun loose last evening. "Take a look," he suggested, "and tell me if you see what I think I do—on that far yonder wall, quite a bit to the north."

Stella left off what she was doing. Close at his side, she tried to follow the direction he indicated. "Can you make it out? A slanting line, along the face of the rock. Almost like it had been scratched with a knifeblade . . ."

With the gulch still swimming in the night mists, and sunlight on the rims, distances could be deceptive; but perhaps at no other hour would the light have fallen in just the right way to point up the thing he had seen. Stella said slowly, "Yes, I think I see. What do you make of it?"

"Nothing, maybe. Could be a short fault line. But somehow I have an idea it's a trail going up the wall of the gulch. It could be our way out."

Stella frowned as she considered, hands busy again looping the braids about her head and pinning it in place. "Won't a trail be guarded?"

"If they think about it, or figure there's any likelihood of our stumbling onto it." He rubbed a palm across his cheeks, which were stiff with yellow beard stubble. "But it seems to me we got to look into this, because I don't see any other possibility at the moment. It means making our way up the gulch somehow, and getting across the creek—"

"And keeping away from Wes Dodd, and the Cagles, while we're about it?" Stella finished.

Bannister nodded grimly. "We might as well get started!"

She thrust the last pin in place, gave a final touch to her hair, then looked down at herself, ruefully smoothing the bedraggled wreckage of her skirt. "Yes," Stella said. "We might just as well . . ."

• • •

Daylight descended with them as the rising sun shot its rays deeper into the gulch, first gilding treeheads and afterward reaching the earth that had been blackened by the night's rainfall and now gave up tendrils of steam. The sun's touch was pleasant, helping to thaw some of the long night's discomfort; then broken clouds, shuttling overhead, would throw the thick timber stands into gloom and they would find themselves shivering once more. Bannister chose their way carefully, holding his pace down out of regard for the woman toiling gamely after him—well aware too that the danger increased as they went deeper into the heart of the gulch.

He was worried about Stella. Even after rest and fitful sleep, it was a question how long she could hold out. Just now hunger was a problem. Neither had actually managed to eat very much last evening at the stage station; and that had been long hours ago. Jim Bannister had grown accustomed, when food wasn't available, to pulling his belt up a notch and managing without. But it was an unfamiliar experience for the woman, and it would be a hardship as she continued to use up her strength.

Slowly and cautiously, they worked their way toward lower country, forced to scramble over a pileup of rock talus before they reached the first trees. Even here the needle pack was slick and to keep their feet they occasionally had to hand themselves down, sliding from trunk to trunk, until the ground began to level out to a degree. Hampered as he was by the shackles, Bannister could offer Stella only occasional help, at the worst places; mostly for her sake he made frequent stops to rest.

Presently, however, he fell into a faintly marked path that he took to be a game trail, which apparently was also used by humans, and he determined to follow it even though he knew the risk. In spite of the danger they had to get down to more negotiable terrain and this looked like the quickest route; traveling blind as they were couldn't gain them anything, and would only wear them out.

The stock trail, sure enough, took them down by easy stages on to a spur where, a couple of times, Bannister was able to get a glimpse below them of the creek twisting like a silver snake. Presently the trail dropped into a ravine that widened and deepened, and there it became more clearly marked, with increasing signs of use. Bannister's feeling of danger sharpened.

Stella asked suddenly, "Do you smell something?"

He had just caught it, himself—an odd, sweetish odor, carried on a vagrant breath of wind and as quickly gone again. He was sure of what it meant, and he turned quickly with a gesture that motioned Stella down; as she dropped at once to her knees behind a shielding manzanita, her glance searched his face for an explanation.

"Stay here," he said. "I want to look into this. . . ." He left her and started off through the brush and trees, moving with real caution and scouting the wind for a recurrence of the taint he had caught before.

The still sat in a hollow, remote and well hidden—Bannister didn't know any reason why these people would be fearful of revenue agents, but probably they'd formed secretive habits back in whatever hill country they came from, and they clung to old ways even where there was no real sense to them. They'd fashioned their still from a patchwork of odds and ends; only the bright copper screw might have been bought outside for the purpose, and Bannister wondered who had had the job of packing it in, on mules, over the narrow switchbacks. In the quiet air of the hollow, the smell of fermenting mash hung heavy.

Bannister had only a limited view from where he stood, hidden in the fringe of timber; but now there were men's voices—a sudden burst of quarreling, so close beyond a bulge of ground that it gave him a start. He counted three, and though they quickly subsided he had heard enough to give him warning. Troubled, he cautiously withdrew, and made his way back to report to an anxiously waiting Stella.

"Do we dare go on?" she exclaimed. "Knowing there are three of them behind us?"

"We can't turn back," he pointed out. "This is the only trail we've found. Those men at the still aren't looking for us—they're busy with whatever it is they're doing. Getting drunk, I imagine. We can just hope they stay at it awhile."

She never questioned his judgment. "Whatever you say, Jim."

"I say we go on . . ."

Yet it was against all his instincts, to leave potential enemies at his back while working his way in unfamiliar territory. As he moved ahead, he knew too much of his thought was still focused on that scene at the still; and that in itself could be dangerous, if it dulled his attention to whatever lay around the next twist of timber-choked trail.

By now the ravine had opened out and was less steep than it had been, so he could guess they were nearing the floor of the gulch. The timber and brush grew sparser. Little more than a quarter mile beyond the hollow where the still was located, the trail made an abrupt turn around a granite outcrop and suddenly a cabin showed before them.

Bannister was not caught by surprise; he had supposed whoever owned the still probably lived near it. He caught Stella's arm and drew her quickly down into the protection of a fallen log. He could hear her shallow breathing, almost feel the tension in her as she crouched close beside him.

The high sun shone directly into his eyes, hampering his vision. Bannister cupped both palms to shade them. It was the first time he'd seen one of these Cagle places by daylight. The cabin sat at the edge of timber on a shallow bench with the creek, probably, just beyond; its windows would command a full view of the descending trail. It was a sway-backed affair, of unpeeled and untrimmed logs whose ends had never been evened off. The roof, steeply pitched, seemed made in equal parts of cedar shakes and flattened tins. A pencil line of smoke rose from the mud-and-stick chimney, to give warning someone was home.

He looked for dogs but didn't see them—nor, unfortunately, anything in the way of a horse he might be able to borrow. Instead a number of scrawny chickens scratched at the dirt and a strutting rooster shook out its feathers and crowed thinly in the warm morning. There were kids, also, playing in the dooryard—three of them, so ragged and unkempt he would have been hard put to tell what sex they were supposed to be.

Finally, there was the woman.

She was hoeing a vegetable patch, and it was

the flash of the blade that caught Bannister's eye. From here she looked as thin and underfed as her chickens, a gaunt figure in a shapeless dress who stooped and straightened, mechanically, as she moved along the rows. He noticed the wooden bucket that seemed to be her sole means of bringing water up from the creek.

Jim Bannister swore silently. The woman herself looked harmless enough, but the men at the still behind them were hardly out of earshot; it worried him to be caught between. Stella, too, understood the problem. She asked in an anxious whisper, "Is there any way we can get past without her seeing, and spreading the alarm?"

"I don't know."

As they watched, the woman put the hoe aside and, straightening up, sleeved sweat from her face. She stood like that, resting from her backbreaking labor while her gaze seemed to travel past their hiding place and on up to the high rim of the gulch. After a long moment she turned away. She left the hoe lying on the ground and started toward the cabin, moving stiffly as though every muscle ached. When she disappeared inside, only the kids and the chickens remained.

Frowning, Bannister considered the situation with impatience eating at him. He supposed they might be able to bypass this place by swinging south through the timber, but it would take them a deal closer to the cabin than he liked; besides, the trees appeared to play out just beyond it, and there was much too good a chance of them being seen.

He used up valuable minutes looking out for some other route but couldn't find one. Aware of the time they were wasting here, he shook his head and told Stella, "I see no option. I guess we'll have to try it through the trees."

"All right," she said.

And then the woman's voice, with the unmistakable twang of the Cagles in it, spoke startlingly, just behind them. "You kin stay sot," it warned, "till I tell you!"

Bannister froze, for a timeless instant; after that, in spite of the warning he couldn't have stopped himself from twisting about. He found himself staring into the twin snouts of an ugly-looking shotgun pointed directly at his face. The woman stood barefooted, in her faded rag of a dress, the weapon braced against one bony hip. Her own face, now that he could see it, probably should have been a fairly young one, but life and toil had aged her. The hair, pulled severely into a bun, was streaked with gray; the eyes were faded, the cheeks gaunt, the mouth settled into a scowl that was probably habitual.

"You be mindful!" she told him harshly. "This thing has got a double charge of buck!"

The shotgun was an ancient one; the stock looked to be held together with old baling wire. But Bannister saw no reason to doubt it could blast a hole through the middle of a man. "Whoever you air," she added through those tight-pressed lips, "you best have a good reason for sneakin' around like you been!"

Bannister's own mouth had gone dry. He wet his lips, trying to think of words. He could feel Stella's eyes on him, and he knew she was wondering if he was going to find another lie for this emergency. He had a bitter feeling it was one situation he could not talk his way out of.

"Ma'am," he said, "I can promise you we mean to do no harm, to you or your children."

"And you sure ain't gonna get the chance, air you?" she retorted. Her pale eyes narrowed. "What's them?" she demanded sharply, and pointed with the muzzle of the shotgun. Bannister looked down, saw she was staring at the manacles. "Them's *handcuffs!*" the woman exclaimed, answering her own question. "They puts 'em onto criminals!"

And she gripped the weapon tighter, knuckles showing white through brown and dirty skin. "So *that's* what I seen shinin', that told me somebody was up here!"

Bannister realized, then, he'd forgotten all about the manacles when he shaded his eyes for a better look at the cabin below him; it simply hadn't occurred to him the smear of sunlight on metal might signal his presence. Having seen it, the woman had calmly quit her hoeing, gone to the cabin for a gun, and left by another door to circle through the timber and surprise him, while he was still futilely debating his own next move.

He had to admire such nerve and toughness; it also taught him a good reason to respect the ancient weapon and the steady, toil-hardened hands that held it leveled on him. He drew a breath. "What do you intend doing with us?"

"One thing, I hain't standin' here jawin' about it," she told him bluntly. "So, git up from there and start walkin' ahead of me. If you git any notions—well, I wouldn't if I was you!"

"No, ma'am."

He had to help Stella to her feet—she was trembling badly, whether from exhaustion or fear of that ugly weapon. No one spoke after that, while the woman marched them down the trail at shotgun point, past the vegetable patch with the abandoned hoe, its blade gleaming in the sunlight, and directly to the cabin dooryard; there, she ordered a halt.

At close hand the squalor of the place was glaringly evident, and yet Bannister noticed a few bedraggled flowers growing along the front of the shack—set out and tended by the woman, he supposed, to try to keep alive some touch of beauty. She'd have had no more support with that, probably, than with the vegetable patch where she had been laboring all alone while her menfolk drank and quarreled at their still.

The children turned out to be two boys and a girl, each of them a Cagle in miniature—rawboned, dishfaced, pale-eyed. They quit their roughhousing to stare at the strangers, who were very possibly the first they'd ever seen. Even the hens stopped scratching. Singling out the oldest boy, his mother snapped an order: "Rupe, you git up the holler and tell your pa and them others to fetch their lazy tails down here, quick!" The boy nodded and went off on his mission without an argument, but he kept a wide-eyed look turned on the prisoners as long as he was able.

Jim Bannister knew time was closing in, but standing there in the sun with his arms raised, and that ugly, wired-together shotgun leveled in the woman's competent hands, he saw very little chance of using what few minutes were left him. A glance at Stella showed the same desperate thought reflected in her eyes. Turning back to the woman he made a last effort.

"Ma'am," he said earnestly, "there'd be no use trying to explain who we are and what kind of trouble we're in. I'll only say again, I meant what I told you—we don't wish harm to anyone. If you could try to believe that—"

She remained as firmly suspicious as ever. "You ain't said yet," she reminded him, "who put them things on your wrists. They don't do that, without somebody's broke the law—and here in the gulch, whatever else we may be weuns is lawabidin'. As for *her*"—the woman nodded toward Stella, who had moved away a little distance and was letting herself down, with a look of pure exhaustion, onto the edge of a chopping block—"I don't know why she's with you, and she looks just about done in; but I cain't see how I can help that any."

Bannister all but forgot his own predicament in sudden alarm for Stella. "Can't you do something for her?" he exclaimed. "It's been an ordeal. For one thing, she's nearly starved. If you have some food, I can pay . . ."

Mention of money seemed to have its effect on a woman who looked as though she all too seldom got her hands on any; besides, he thought her frown showed genuine feeling for another woman in distress. But she hesitated only a moment. Male dominance was the keynote of this Cagle clan, apparently, for she shook her head and told him, "I guess we'll wait and find out what the mister says. The boy'll be back with him in a minute, I reckon."

And then it would be too late. Even if some of these people hadn't learned yet about the manhunt, they probably would soon enough; and until then, the mere fact of being strangers should be enough to decide them to hang onto the prisoners the woman had taken. Bannister gritted his teeth in sheer frustration.

A movement from Stella brought his glance to her again. She seemed to have found her strength while the other two were talking, and now was getting back to her feet. The woman must have caught this out of a corner of her eye. All at once she seemed aware that she'd let herself be outmaneuvered; for she took a hasty step back and belatedly tried to bring the shotgun to bear on both prisoners at once. "You, lady!" she said sharply. "You best git over there with your man . . ."

Stella eyed the shotgun, and then her glance lifted and sought Bannister's and he read the message she flashed him, realizing that she had behaved with a deliberate purpose. He saw now it was a desperate chance she offered, but with no better choice he took it.

He gave her a tight nod to show he understood, and then he was starting forward, directly toward the woman with the shotgun.

CHAPTER IX

At once she turned, catlike, swinging the weapon around. Bannister dived for the earth; he hit hard, rolling as he fell, and heard the thunderous roar of the shotgun and a rush of buckshot that could have blown him in two. Instead it drilled empty air where he had been standing a split second earlier. He almost thought he felt the heat of the muzzle blast. Earth and sky blurred; a sharp tang of powdersmoke, that mingled with the smell of rain-damp earth, clogged his nostrils.

Coughing on it, and with hearing numbed, he caught himself on one elbow and searched for the woman through the fog of smoke—he remembered she still had one charge left, unfired. He saw her then; she had been staggered by the recoil. And as she recovered and braced herself to fire again, Bannister to his horror saw Stella Harbord moving in, reaching to grab the shotgun.

Only the smoke clogging his throat prevented him crying out involuntarily. At the last moment the Cagle woman became aware of a new danger. Just as she turned Stella collided with her, the impact snapping her head on her shoulders; the shotgun's second barrel was touched off but it exploded harmlessly at the sky. After that, the women were down in a tangle.

Bannister came blundering to his feet, fear for Stella making his legs tremble. He felt a rushing relief, then, to see she had rolled clear. The other woman lay where she'd fallen, her back arched and her weathered face stretched into a grimace—mouth agape, eyes straining wide.

Already, through the ringing echoes of the twin blasts that numbed his ears, Jim Bannister could hear distant shouting; the men from the still were coming, at a run. He got to Stella, on her knees now, and took her by an arm. "We have to get out of here!"

She held back, staring at the figure writhing on the ground. "What have I *done* to her?" she cried. "Poor thing—she looks half starved, herself. And to go up there after us, like that—alone: That took real grit and courage!"

Bannister nodded. "But we've got to think about ourselves . . ."

The children in their crude homespuns stood looking on, hand-in-hand and wide-eyed. It was the girl who said, in a matter-of-fact tone, "You never hurt Ma none, lady. She just windied herself, when the shotgun kicked her."

A closer look showed Bannister the girl was correct. Her mother was gasping convulsively, diaphragm muscles struggling to refill emptied lungs. "She's called it," he told Stella. "The woman will be all right. But we're in trouble if we don't move. Look!"

Running figures had burst into sight, above them on the slope—two, and then a third. Quickly Bannister hauled Stella to her feet and pointed her at the nearest timber. She seemed to stumble, dropping briefly on one knee; then she was up again and Bannister led her away at a run, while up there on the slope someone raised a shout. After that they had left the shack behind them, the woman and the kids and the chickens, and a moment later the shadow of the trees closed overhead.

Jim Bannister, turning to wait for Stella, saw her laboring after him and realized she hadn't really stumbled—instead, she'd deliberately taken time to stoop and snatch up the empty shotgun. It was a cumbersome weight, and no real use without shells; nevertheless, Bannister had to admire her quick thinking, no less than the rare courage with which she'd tackled that woman and thereby saved them both, when he himself could only stand helplessly staring into the shotgun's muzzle. But, he'd always known Stella Harbord was no ordinary woman.

He relieved her of the weapon now, was about to fling it away when an obscure impulse made him keep hold of it and carry it at high port in his manacled grasp. Even an empty gun beat none at all.

They ran on, Stella managing as well as she could with bedraggled skirts that clung to her legs and threatened constantly to trip her. Bannister could hear her labored breathing. Because of their own noise it was hard to judge if the men from the still were coming after them, but he couldn't doubt it.

Every Cagle he'd met so far was hostile to strangers—and these three had been drinking.

The trees didn't promise much in the way of cover—only some scattered pine and aspen spilling down out of a draw. An open stretch lay beyond, studded with boulders. While Bannister halted to size up the problem, Stella let herself sag against a tree trunk where she sobbed for breath, numbly waiting for him to reach a decision.

Not far from where they stood, a plummeting boulder had some time or other knocked down a small stand of pine saplings. They lay in a tangle, their trunks stripped of bark and turning gray with age, and buck brush had grown up in a kind of screen. It wasn't much, but Bannister touched Stella's arm and pointed.

It took them only moments to get into hiding. The space was cramped, barely cover enough for the two of them. They fitted themselves to it, keeping their heads down, as they crouched in the dirt and welcomed a chance to settle their breathing.

Stella's face, so close to Bannister's, was shining with sweat and dirt-smeared, with a trace of blood where a broken branch had raked her forehead. "Are you all right?" he demanded anxiously. "Believe me! When I saw you charge that shotgun—!"

She made a rather unsuccessful attempt to smile, the pupils of her eyes so dilated with excitement as to make them appear almost black. "I thought I saw a chance," she said. "I didn't think about being scared until afterward."

"I knew you had courage," Bannister said gravely. "But until today I never realized—" And then he broke off and laid a warning finger to her lips. They froze as hurrying footsteps approached their hiding place.

It sounded like a couple of them out there. They came to a halt, as though searching for some sign of the fugitives, and one said in a high nasal voice, "By God, if your Marthy was a drinkin' woman I'd say it was all in her head! A man and a woman—and the man wearin' wrist irons. Now, if that ain't the wildest yarn I ever heared!"

"We seen 'em," the second man pointed out.

"*You* seen 'em, you told me. I never. And I know what *you* was drinkin'!"

Marthy's husband swore roughly. And now, off in the trees somewhere, a third voice shouted something. Bannister couldn't make it out, but one of the pair called back, "No, nothin' here at all."

Another shout—this time, faintly, Bannister

made out part of it: "—and I'll cut north and look around Saddle Rock . . ."

"You do that . . . I think I'll see if they headed for the creek," the man went on, to his companion. "Why don't you foller up this draw a piece? If we neither of us pick up anything, then we best get word through the gulch so's the rest can start lookin'. We cain't let 'em get away."

The other mumbled an agreement and after that there was the sound of them moving off; the thud of boots faded, stillness settled again over the patch of wood.

"That was a little too close!" Jim Bannister said.

Stella found her voice. "What do we do now?"

"Give them a minute to spread out. We don't want to move too soon."

Deeply troubled, she asked, "What do you suppose will happen if they catch us?"

He shook his head. "Hard to say. It's plain they haven't heard from Wes Dodd. Are they worked up because they found us snooping— or only because these are hill people, and we're strangers?" He paused, frowning. "Or, is it something else altogether, that's got them so anxious?"

"What do you mean?"

"I'm not sure I know. Just a feeling I have . . ." He shrugged. "But being taken by them," he added grimly, "is hardly any better than falling into Wes Dodd's hands—and there's too good a chance that's just where it would end."

They thought about that as they listened to the continuing stillness—the hum of wind in pine branches, and somewhere behind it the distant noise of the creek. A squirrel discovered their hiding place and scolded them briefly from a limb overhead, before it whisked away.

Stella said presently, "I don't hear anybody now."

"Me, either." Bannister, grown impatient with waiting, reached a decision. "I'm going to have a look around," he said. "I won't be long . . ."

For whatever use it might be to him, he took the empty shotgun. Ghosting from tree to tree, he made little sound in the litter of pine needles that carpeted the draw. As he went lower the draw widened and the trees grew thinner. He came at last to a halt with the creek, itself, in front of him.

A horse trail followed the bank—obviously, a route by which Cagles passed up and down the gulch between their separate holdings, strung along its length. Just now the trail lay empty, from where it broke out of a growth of willow, upstream, until it curved around a knob of rock that crowded the creek bank on his right. That knob restricted his view but it also suggested a vantage point. On impulse he turned to it.

It was no difficult climb, even with shackled hands. As he approached the top, Bannister kept low, to avoid skylining himself, and was rewarded for his effort by a good overlook of this stretch of the canyon. The creek tumbled through it, here, with a fairly stiff current, along a course partly choked with logs and boulders. Upstream there was no immediate sign of habitation; but just below him was the log shanty on its bench above the creek, where he and Stella had confronted the woman with her shotgun. Now Bannister tensed as he discovered the trio of riders who were sitting their horses in the sun, before the door.

They were close enough that he had no trouble making them out. The one wearing a corduroy jacket, high polished boots, and a narrow-brimmed hat could only be Wes Dodd; the larger of the remaining pair looked like Vern Cagle, from here. The other would be his cousin Dewey.

Breath ran shallow in his chest as he lay watching. Wind along the bench whipped the horses' tails; it caught at the skirts of the woman, Marthy, where she stood talking to the riders with her head tilted and an arm lifted against the sun's glare. Bannister didn't think he needed to be told just what they were talking about.

Now the woman pointed toward the trees—probably, he thought, indicating the place where she'd seen Bannister and Stella disappear. Without waiting for more, Vern and Dewey Cagle spun their horses and sent them lunging off in that direction; but Wes Dodd hung back. There was further exchange with the woman. They seemed to be interested now in the trail that, running past the cabin, dropped off the bench toward the creek. After a moment Dodd touched finger to hat brim and reined away, leaving her standing there. But instead of following the Cagles, he swung toward the creek trail, and there was a glance of sunlight on metal when he brought his gun from under his coat.

Bannister's mouth tightened. Obviously the manhunter was thinking ahead; if his two helpers succeeded in flushing the quarry and driving them toward the creek, then Wes Dodd meant to be on hand to pin them down. . . . Eyes narrowing, Jim Bannister toyed with the idea that had just occurred to him. He weighed the odds, examined the risk, and quickly made up his mind. But there was no time to waste. Moving fast, now, he turned and half scrambled, half slid from his post atop the knob of rock.

The last few yards he took a spill, rolling and landing heavily, just managing to catch himself on his two manacled hands. He had dropped the shotgun in the fall—but when he saw where it had fallen, a short distance away, he got to it and snatched the weapon up—barely in time. The rider was approaching along the narrow creekbank, hoofbeats audible now above the racket of the water. Bannister set himself, waiting. A moment later Wes Dodd came around the foot of the big rock, almost on top of the other man before he saw him.

At the last moment, remembering the gun he had seen in Dodd's hand, Jim Bannister gave up any plan of trying a bluff with the empty shotgun. He reversed his grip, holding the weapon by the barrel like a club, and it was as a club that he used it. He saw the manhunter's quick turn of head, even saw the look on his face as Dodd caught a glimpse of him there beside the trail. Dodd's whole body seemed to stiffen; the short gun in his hand started to come up.

The shotgun's barrels blurred reflected light as Bannister put all the weight of his shoulders, and the thrust of a forward step, behind the swing. The wooden stock came around and took Wes Dodd squarely in the chest. Bannister felt the shock of collision; in the same instant, startlingly, wood split and baling wire snapped and the ancient tied-together weapon simply came apart in his hands. Above his head, Dodd's gun smashed a shot; but it must have been a reflex movement of the man's thumb sliding off the hammer flange, for the bullet went wide. Ears ringing, hands numbed, Bannister stumbled under the momentum of his own violent movement. He caught himself, and then he was tossing aside the metal tubes that were all that remained of the shotgun, as he saw Wes Dodd drop backward from the saddle.

The horse leaped ahead with a snort of terror. Bannister gave a lunge, attempting to trap the animal's reins. Had his hands been free he might have made it, but the manacles hampered him—one leather strap flicked across the ends of his fingers. Then a muscled haunch struck him a solid blow and drove him off his feet, and the horse was gone. He had lost his hat, taking a knock on the head that stunned him; he got to hands and knees but with daylight pulsing to the throb of his heartbeat he could only crouch there, and wait until his head cleared. After that, on his feet again, he stumbled a little as he made his way back to where Dodd lay sprawled.

The manhunter was unconscious. Bannister went shakily to his knees. He saw the handgun Dodd had dropped; smoke trailed from its muzzle as he snatched it up. It held four unfired shells—but unluckily, not the same calibre as the ones in his holster belt. He laid it aside and made a search of the unconscious man's clothing, hoping to find his own sixshooter that had been taken from him down at the stage station.

There was no sign of it, nor of the rifle Dodd must have discarded as too cumbersome to manage without a saddle scabbard. Bitterly disappointed, he sank back on his heels; most likely his revolver was in a saddle pocket on the horse that had got away from him—and Bannister swore a little, thinking how near he'd come to capturing it.

Wes Dodd was groaning now, commencing to stir. That reminded Bannister of one more thing he wanted from him, and he began a more careful search of the man's pockets. At last, stuck in the lining of the corduroy jacket, he felt the piece of steel he was looking for. Hastily he dug it out and set to work at once trying to unfasten the handcuffs.

He was too eager. The key slipped from his fingers, and lost itself for a frightening instant in wire grass that grew thick on the creek bank; he hunted with a touch of panic before he found it again. Just as he did so, he became aware of voices.

Sunlight stabbed at his eyes, as he raised his head to listen. Something told him that wasn't only Vern and Dewey who were coming—the men from the still, too, were sure to have heard that single gunshot. In any event, they were far too many for him. Bannister came to his feet, snatching up the gun with the four loaded cylinders, and looked for the nearest cover.

That would be the growth of scrub, at the rock knob's base. It wasn't much at best, but he had no time to look farther; as it was, he had scarcely got into it when the first rider went spurring past, within yards of him: Vern Cagle, and right on his heels his cousin, Dewey. Moments later another of the Cagles showed, this one afoot— perhaps the husband of Marthy, and the sire of those starved-looking youngsters at the cabin. He yelled something but apparently the horsemen didn't hear him; getting no answer he went after them at a run toward the creek, a long-barreled hogleg pistol swinging from the end of one arm.

As soon as he passed, Bannister was ready to go. By eye-estimate, an open of some twenty yards separated him from the better protection of the trees, but whatever the risks he knew he was trapped if he stayed where he was. He broke from his hiding place and started, prepared at the first shout to halt, and turn, and defend himself with the captured revolver.

A confusion of sound rose now from the excited men on the creek bank behind him, but the seconds passed with nothing to show he had been discovered. It was a good deal like running in a nightmare—for all his effort the trees didn't seem to get closer. Yet abruptly he was there; he hauled up in the shadows, panting. And while he had a moment, he slid the gun into his holster and—not hurrying now, forcing himself to take his time—made one more try with the key.

This time he was able to get it properly inserted. The lock clicked; the steel band sprang open. He was quickly free.

Bannister's first impulse was to fling the

shackles as far as he could throw them; instead, he shoved handcuffs and key into a hip pocket and, standing there in the warm wind that funneled along the draw, massaged his wrists. He winced at the raw chafing, and yet the pain felt good since it told him that now—for the first time since those manacles snapped into place—he was more or less in command of his own destiny.

And with a gun in his holster, he told himself with bleak satisfaction, he was at least in a position to fight back. . . .

CHAPTER X

It felt, Wes Dodd told them, as though the wild swing of that shotgun stock had crushed every bone in his chest. He walked about, still in something of a daze, hunch-shouldered and wincing with pain at each breath he took. A livid bruise was shaping up, but his exploring touch seemed to find no actual broken ribs. He was short tempered and when Dewey came spurring back, leading the roan horse that he'd caught up, Dodd thanked him with no more than a nod.

The Cagles—five of them now, gathered on the mud bank—had already refused any suggestion they should go after the fugitive. "Not a chance!" one of them said flatly. "I ain't lost no train robber in *that* timber—not if he's got him a gun! Mister, if you want him you can look for him."

"Hain't likely he'd still be in there, nohow," another pointed out. "The time he's had."

Dodd looked at them in angry disgust, but he saw no point in arguing. Instead he demanded, "Where could the man go?"

"Lots of places," Vern Cagle told him. "Country roughs up, farther upstream you travel. Even a stranger wouldn't have it too hard, keepin' out of sight."

"Is there a place where he can climb out of the gulch?"

Vern shook his head. "Only one that I ever heard of and he wouldn't know about it. Naw, it's just a matter of diggin' him out—and not give him the chance to kill too many of us in the meanwhile. Hit maybe could take some time."

Wes Dodd swore, temper shortened by the bruising pain that stabbed at him whenever he happened to make an incautious move. Now Dewey Cagle came toward him, with a battered black hat he had picked up from the ground. "Look here. The feller lost something . . ."

"Give me that!"

Dodd snatched the hat and stood turning it in his hands, scowling. Vern said, "It's his'n, all right. He was a-wearin' it when you brung him into the station."

The manhunter turned on him, spurred by a sudden thought. "Those stupid dogs," he said quickly. "Could they pick up a trail, given a scent to work from?"

"Usin' the hat, you mean?" Vern Cagle shrugged. "Cousin Heck swears by old Spoon, give him half a chance."

"Then we'll give him one. Go get the dogs."

"Well, now—I just dunno. After how you talked about 'em last night, Heck might not—"

"Get them!" Dodd ordered, sharply. "And quick! This manhunt is taking too damn much time. What your cousin happens to think of the way I talk is the last thing that concerns me right now."

"Whatever you say," Vern Cagle told him and turned to his horse. Mounted, he held it on the rein a moment as he looked coldly at the manhunter. "Maybe it never occurred to you, mister, but us Cagles got our pride. Still, I'll see if I can persuade him."

He rode off down the creek.

When he neared the place where he had left Stella Harbord, Bannister actually thought she had disobeyed his orders. The silence was complete. He called her name once, as loudly as he dared, but got no answer. Alarmed, he hurried forward—and there she was, a huddled figure in the space behind the fallen logs, face buried in her arms. She looked so vulnerable that he stood a moment and looked at her, engulfed with love and tenderness and pity. Then he spoke her name again, gently, and dropped down beside her.

She lifted a face that was drawn, and streaked with dirt and tears. At first she stared as though not believing she really saw him; then with a cry she threw herself into his arms, and she was shaking. He heard her muffled voice: "I heard a shot! I—I just knew—"

Bannister held her, letting her have it out. The trembling slowly passed. She pushed away from him then, wiping her wet cheeks with her palms; she was herself again, and in a normal tone she asked, "What did happen?"

"As a matter of fact," he said, "I didn't do too badly. I've got myself a gun, with four bullets in it. And even more than that—look!"

She hadn't noticed that his hands were free. As she stared at them he told her briefly of the encounter on the creekbank. "Oh, Jim!" she exclaimed. "Wasn't that a terrible risk? Confronting that man Dodd, with nothing, but an empty shotgun!"

"It paid off. So I can't complain, even though I didn't get the horse—that's what I was really after."

"What do we do now?"

"Get moving," he answered. "At once! That gunshot has drawn in all the men who were hunting us, so for the moment at least—until they spread out again—we should have a clear field."

Stella suggested, "Do you suppose we should turn back? We know what's behind us, but there's no telling what lies the other way."

"No telling, either," he pointed out, "what kind of storm Dodd may have already stirred up. If we keep going, at least we can hope to stay ahead of whatever word he's spreading."

"Yes, I suppose you're right . . ."

Bannister chose a course for them, through the boulder field stretching north of this tree-choked draw. Stella having had some rest, he could set a stiffer pace. Still reveling in the sensation of having both hands free, he felt almost good enough to ignore the hunger pangs he knew were plaguing them both.

The gulch seemed to be narrowing; Bannister supposed they would soon find themselves crowded in ever nearer toward its center. But that was in his plans anyway, since he was still bound on investigating what had looked like a trail up the opposite wall. Crossing the creek would be the moment of greatest peril, but he saw no way to avoid that.

So at length he began deliberately moving back down toward the creek; its voice, when they picked it up, seemed to hold almost an angry note. Presently they brought it in sight and found it had grown a good deal narrower, and more turbulent. Where it foamed over sunken boulders, or broke against a half-drowned log, a spray of white water was flung high in the sun to flash like jewels. The noise of its churning rush came up to them, amplified by the sounding board of high rock walls.

Jim Bannister felt Stella's hand tighten on his. It wasn't hard to read her thoughts; he glanced into her anxious face and told her, reassuringly, "It's all right. We'll find a way over."

Shortly after, he located an old deer trail that made for an easier descent. Caution was high in him as they began to approach the canyon bottom; when some small animal broke and bolted away through crackling brush, the gun leaped from his holster and he waited out tense moments while his nerves settled, going on again only when he was certain no one waited up ahead.

The creek's damp breath was in their faces as they emerged at last upon the muddy bank; the pound of white water smashing against a sunken log seemed to make the ground tremble, and blanketed their voices. After checking directions, Bannister motioned to the woman and led off along the creek trail, working upstream in a search for quieter water.

He suspected there was no way they were going to get across without getting wet.

A few yards above a boiling miniature rapids, a deeper pool opened where a log had dammed up the swirling flow of water; here the noise slackened enough that they could actually hear each other's voices. And here Stella paused beside the wreckage of a crude, boxlike construction, made of whipsawed lumber gray with weathering, that lay half-hidden in the willow growth. "What do you suppose it is?" she asked.

Bannister gave the thing a nudge with a boot toe, and the ancient lumber wobbled and fell apart. "A gold rocker," he said. "Or, what's left of it. I've noticed signs that this creek has been worked, one time or another. Maybe it was the Cagles, maybe somebody that came before them."

"Do you think they found anything?"

"Not much, anyway, or they'd have worked it a lot more than this. After all, there isn't an inch of these mountains that wasn't prospected over, at one time or another in the past twenty years. A lot of places yielded color, but little else."

"It makes you wonder, more than ever," Stella observed, "why these people stay. The winters must be really terrible, and what crops they grow can hardly do more than—"

A lift of his hand silenced her. She looked at him, puzzled; then her eyes widened in quick apprehension.

The bugling of hounds on a scent, once heard, wasn't a sound likely to be forgotten. As they listened, now, the sound swelled and echoed off the walls of the gulch—a wild music, in which Bannister could begin to sort out the separate voices. More than two this time, he thought. Last night, hunting a trail they couldn't find, they had been anxious and whining with frustration. Now there was triumphant eagerness, and Jim Bannister said grimly, "They're onto something—and I guess there's no question that it's us!"

Stella cried, "They're getting closer!"

"By the minute!" Bannister took her by the

arm, and turned her toward the water. "And only one way to lose them." He pointed. "We'll angle upstream toward that snag lying in the water, on the far side. That should help break the current.

"Follow me, and keep close." He led the way over the rocky bank, into the creek.

The shocking chill of the water took away one's breath; after the first steps it was clear they were in trouble. This pool was deeper than it looked, and treacherous beneath its placid surface. Jim Bannister felt the clutch of the current at his ankles, heard Stella's gasp as it hit her. Across a shoulder he shouted, "Grab my belt!" She had to reach for it. He waited until he knew she had a firm grip; then, drawing his gun to keep it from a soaking, he commenced wading upstream, holding close to the bank until they were nearly opposite the snag. "Now!" Bannister said, and turned toward it.

The instant they had got away from the bank, the bottom, treacherously floored here with jagged rocks, dropped until he was in to his hips; he had to brace himself for each step against the rush of icy water. He knew that Stella—in above her waist, hampered by her full skirt—must really be struggling now.

Constantly, the racket of the hounds grew louder to remind them how close their enemies were.

Fighting for each step, Bannister was almost

in reach of the snag when he felt the grip on his belt torn loose. He looked around to see Stella being carried under. He grabbed for her, caught hold of her clothing, but in so doing lost his own footing. His legs were swept from under him, the frigid waters closed briefly over his head. In the next instant he broke surface again, head ringing with the pressure on his eardrums. Still keeping his grip on Stella, he flung his other arm out; handicapped by the revolver that he still held, he was just able to hook his wrist over the top of the snag. He got his boots under him. Hanging onto the snag, he pulled Stella up and set her on her feet.

She could only cling to him, coughing and retching. Not hesitating, Bannister leaned, lifted her across a shoulder, and made his way up the steep bank, slipping to his knees once before he could put her down. Casting about, he saw a jumble of boulders and said quickly, "That way! Hurry!"

But when she tried to obey, she stumbled and would have fallen if he hadn't caught her. After his submersion he was able to hear nothing at all, just then—neither the creek, nor the baying hounds, nor Stella's anguished cry as she clutched at him to steady herself. But he saw her expression, and her mouth formed the words: "My ankle . . ." Quickly pouching his revolver, he took her under knees and shoulders and hurried with her up the bank toward the rocks. He rounded them and dropped to his knees. Crouched there, soaked and shivering, they both worked to clear water from their throats and recover the ability to breathe.

Bannister's hearing returned, with a rush. Suddenly there was the wind in the trees overhead, the tumbling of the creek—and now, men's voices mingled with the noise of the dogs. He drew his gun, only hoping the cartridges in the chambers hadn't been submerged long enough to soak the powder. With a hand on Stella's shoulder to reassure her and keep her where she was, he raised himself carefully for a look.

At once he saw the first riders breaking into view, beyond the trees that fringed the farther bank. He made out seven, and immediately recognized Wes Dodd on his roan; two of the others were Vern and Dewey. And, there were the dogs—four, that he counted, and judged that Spoon and Annie had been joined in the hunt by someone else's animals. He watched them stirring the creekside willows, moving in and out of the brush, circling about in a baffled search to pick up the trail they had plainly lost.

The men were angry—their voices carried above the noise of the water, and though he couldn't make out what they said he could tell there was high dissension, probably over the performance of the dogs. Nearly opposite where the fugitives had left the water, they pulled up and Bannister caught his breath as one rider lifted an arm, seeming to point straight at the nest of boulders where he and Stella lay hidden. In that moment he was positive they knew every move he had made; he tensed, thoroughly expecting someone to put his horse into the water, and if the dogs should follow there would quickly be an end to it.

Yet nothing happened, except for some more arm waving and continued debate, during a long, gut-tightening stretch of minutes. Finally, Wes Dodd reined his horse away and sent him along the bank, pushing on upstream. The others fell into line, and the dogs ran faster with noses to ground, tails wagging hopefully. When they had all passed completely from sight, Jim Bannister eased the air from his lungs and discovered he had been clutching the sixshooter so hard his fingers ached. He slid the weapon into leather, and let himself down by Stella's side.

He saw she was shuddering spasmodically, knew this was caused partly by shock and fear but mostly by the thorough soaking she'd endured. He touched her hand, felt the icy chill. He had been immersed completely, too, but only for a second, and his jacket was heavy and thickly lined. He stripped out of it and placed it around her shoulders, for whatever warmth it could give; then took both her hands and rubbed them as he told her encouragingly, "They rode on by; they haven't the slightest idea where we are. We're safe for now."

It was as good a spot as any—completely hidden, the rocks deflecting the wind and at the same time collecting the noon sunlight to hold it as in a cup. Their clothing should dry in short order.

Stella lifted her head. Her lips were blue, her hair undone and straggling. She put up a hand and pushed the wet tangle back from her face, and she said in despair, "But now what happens? I twisted my ankle there in the water. I don't know if I can even hobble."

He made a quick examination. Her right ankle was already a little swollen, and she bit back a cry of pain at his touch. He shook his head. A bad sprain could immobilize a person as completely as a broken bone. Too early to tell yet just how severe this one was.

Bannister swore—and then looked at Stella again and saw the anguish in her face, the unshed tears trembling on her lashes. "I'm sorry!" Her voice shook. "I couldn't help it . . ."

He touched a hand against her cheek, gently. "I wasn't swearing at you—just at this whole damnable situation! I'm losing my patience with it. A man goes along, doing his best, trying to survive without hurting other people even when they're doing all they can to finish him off. But

145

there's limits to what he can take—and damn it, I've reached mine!"

Her stare pinned on his face; she demanded, "What—what are you going to do?"

"Get us out of this," he promised her grimly. "Somehow—whatever it costs! The thing we need worst now is a horse. Somewhere in this gulch, there's one to be had; I mean to get it, right now I don't particularly care how.

"We don't want to try moving you yet," he went on. "Not with that hurt ankle—and this place is probably as safe as any. I'm going to leave you here. No way of knowing how long I'll be gone. I'll be careful—but I won't come back empty-handed!"

Stella studied the determined set of his features. He sensed the protest welling in her, but she held it back. Instead her hand tightened on his, for a long moment; then she let it go, nodding as she said, "All right, Jim. I'll try to be here when you come back."

He bent and kissed her lips, and found them cold. And then he left her.

CHAPTER XI

Bannister knew nothing of the lay of things, here on this east side of the creek, but with the country roughing up as the gulch steepened he thought it unlikely he would find many more of the crude cabins upstream. Besides, the manhunters had ridden that way and he certainly didn't want to run into them; so on quitting his hiding place he started walking south.

The wind that poured along the gulch seemed to cut to the bone, but it soon began to suck moisture from his clothing and the exercise warmed him. His boots, however, were still thoroughly soaked and he was wary of raising blisters, yet he couldn't see any choice but to keep plugging doggedly ahead. He moved cautiously, searching out every twist and turn of the horse trail as it opened before him. His hand was never far from the gun, with its four loads, that he carried in his holster.

He thought he must have been traveling for a good part of an hour, when a blind curve of the trail brought him an unexpected sight that halted him abruptly. What he had found was a green pocket of meadow, set back from the creek and all but hidden from it. It looked like a good spot, sheltered and with a sparkling run of a stream breaking out of pine and aspen; he was not at all surprised, then, to discover still another of the cabins, at the meadow's far end, complete with a barn and other outbuildings. The cabin was an old one. Its logs were weathered, and seemed almost to have settled a little into the ground.

The thing that caught Jim Bannister's eye was the pole corral, with a trio of horses in it.

He stood for several minutes, watching almost hungrily as they moved about in there. The distance was too great to make out anything as to markings or colors, but a horse was what he needed and he couldn't be particular. What did bother him was the thought of taking another man's property—it went against every grain of feeling; but then he thought of Stella, dependent on him, and he thought of all they had had to put up with from these people, and his mouth hardened.

There was no chance of moving in close without being seen, and with a weapon in his holster he didn't try. Rank sawgrass slashed at his boots and his hand was near the gun as he strode forward into the open; his glance busily watched the house and the sheds beyond. If a rifle or a shotgun suddenly appeared at a door or a window, he meant to be ready.

But the place could have been deserted, for any life he could see other than the horses in the pen.

Suddenly he almost paused in his tracks, attention narrowing on one of those animals. It was still too far to distinguish markings or conformations, but to a horseman's trained eye it was all there, in the way it moved, in the lift of its head . . . He knew then, beyond question: This was his own dun.

A man could hardly be wrong about an animal that had carried him that many lonely miles.

In his pleased surprise he almost forgot danger. Meanwhile, the wind at his back apparently carried a familiar scent. All three horses were aware of him, but there was a genuine eagerness in the way the dun stretched its neck over the top bar in greeting, as he covered the last of the distance and held out a hand to it.

Someone said, "Acts almost like he knows you . . ."

Bannister's head jerked about. The man in the cabin doorway looked harmless enough. He had a thinning straggle of white hair, a beard that had been chopped off short across the front of his bib overalls.

Jim Bannister, ready for an argument, said bluntly, "The horse knows me, all right. He happens to belong to me. Got away last night, and I've been hunting him."

The old man considered this, face expressionless. He had the Cagle features, gaunted and hollow-cheeked, dry skin stretched tautly over the bones. He might have been a tall man once, but now he stood slack shouldered and with knees a little bent, as though the weight of years pressed him down. There was no sign of a weapon; his hands hung empty at his sides, and his expression was only mildly curious—perhaps, at his age, nothing was apt to surprise him very much. One eye was milky, obviously sightless.

He said, "A strange horse, and a stranger in the gulch—not too hard to figure they'd go together. Weuns don't see many strangers. They ain't exactly welcome."

"I've had *that* made clear!" Bannister agreed sourly.

"Heard the dogs a-buglin', hour or so ago," the old man went on as though he hadn't spoken. "Somewheres across the creek yonder. Sounded like they was on the trail of something; I figured then they up and lost it again—in the creek, maybe." And his mild stare measured Jim Bannister: hatless, unshaven, still showing the signs of the soaking he'd taken in the turbulent creek water.

Bannister kept a careful hold on his temper, knowing he was being gently needled. He answered shortly, "I heard the dogs. All I'm concerned about is collecting my horse—also my gear, if you've got it." He looked about, hunting his saddle and other belongings. And that was when he gave an involuntary start as he saw the one who stood, motionlessly watching him, at a station near a corner of the cabin.

A moment ago, he had not been there. Bannister had an impression of a stunted shape, of a shaggy and uncombed mop of wild yellow hair, of a splayed nose and a scarred mouth and a pendulous lower lip. That glimpse was all he had; the moment he knew he was being looked at, the other darted back from sight with the manner of a startled wild creature.

The old man explained casually, "That's my grandson Charlie. Hain't too bright, by some thinkin'. I keep him hyere with me on account his folks are dead." He went on to answer the question that the stranger hadn't yet asked: "Charlie found your animal grazing across the creek, early this morning. He knowed it was a strange horse so he brung him home, and I couldn't think what else to do with him but put him in the corral. Gear I took off him is in the shed." He pointed to a leanto structure, near the pen.

Jim Bannister said quickly, "I can identify my stuff. The saddle is a center-fire rig, and there should be a pair of field glasses in a case, strapped to the pommel. In the saddle bags—"

"Hit's your outfit, I reckon," the old man interrupted. "So save your breath. Maybe you wouldn't call us sociable but we're law abidin'— we respect a man's property, and the ordinary notions of right and wrong. Though I *would* be curious," he added thoughtfully, "to hear how you happen to be in this neck of the woods, in the first place." The milky stare rested on him shrewdly. "Don't look like no prospector, and you ain't got none of the traps for it. But nobody else would have much reason to come into country like this."

Bannister shrugged. He tried to make his answer casually convincing. "I'm one that never needed much reason. I see a trail, I'm apt as not to follow it just to see where it goes. Sometimes it proves interesting."

"And sometimes maybe a mite unhealthy?" Something in the mild comment suggested that the old man was still hearing, in his head, the bugling of the dogs across the creek.

"That can help make it interesting," Jim Bannister said, and would be prodded no further. "Appreciate you taking care of the horse. I'll fetch my gear, saddle up, and be riding."

The old man sucked at the inside of a cheek; all at once Bannister had a feeling he might be starved for company, and loath to see the stranger go. "Hit's dinner time. I was jist about to go in and fry me and the boy a mess of 'taters and venison steak. You be welcome to join us."

Mere mention of food was enough to remind Bannister of the hollowness in his belly. He hesitated, seriously tempted; but then he thought of Stella who was no less hungry, and also frightened and alone and waiting out every moment of his absence that must seem like an hour. Reluctantly he told the other, "Much obliged. But I think I better move on."

He found his outfit in the shed, as promised. The blanket roll and the pockets of the saddle bags had been searched but so far as he could tell nothing, not even the glasses prominently strapped to the pommel, had been taken. Which was certainly strange, when you considered the poverty of these people; he'd have expected them to help themselves to anything that fell in their hands. It must be the old man was scrupulously honest—"law-abiding", as he put it—and kept this gear intact with an idea that its owner would, sooner or later, be showing up to claim it.

Carrying his saddle and belongings outside, Bannister brought the dun from the corral and tied it to the fence while he slung the rig in place. Charlie had re-emerged and was standing by at a distance, slacklipped and expressionless, watching the stranger work. His grandfather, whose invitation to a meal had been rejected, came out now to make a further suggestion. "You ain't got much there in the way of vittles. How about I was to hack off a little haunch meat, for you to tote along? Man on the move, he cain't always take time for huntin' game and dressin' it out proper."

Bannister, turning from tightening his cinch, looked at the man. "Now, that's an offer I'll take. And many thanks."

"Step inside, why don't you?" the other said. "I'll see what all I can rustle up." He shouted an order for Charlie to fetch the meat from the cooler, and then led his visitor inside.

It was Bannister's second look at the interior of one of these cabins, and though this one was crude enough, it seemed well built—as it would have to be, to withstand the rigors of Colorado winters. The log walls were of double thickness, no doubt with a layer of earth between. There were a couple of bunks, for the old man and his grandson, and a minimum of home-crafted furniture. A deep stone fireplace served for both cooking and heating.

The old man waved Bannister to a stool and offered him a tin cup of coffee; it was black and bitter from reheating but he welcomed it— it helped to fill some of the void. Bannister commented, above the cup's rim, "You people here likely don't see many outsiders. Kind of a hard life, isn't it?"

"Hit's one we're used to," the other said with a shrug. "Not all that different from the way weuns lived, twenty years gone, back in Missouri."

"You all came out together?"

"That was in 'Sixty-one," the old man said, running fingers through the chopped-off white beard—he appeared to like to talk, and perhaps didn't have the opportunity too often. "Even in the Ozarks we could see Missouri was splittin' in two over the slavery thing, and we never wanted no part of other folks' fuss. And about that time my younger brother Martin, that'd come to Colorado for the Pike's Peak excitement, he writ home and told about this gulch he'd found. Said we'd make our fortunes. To me, hit looked like a chance to hang onto our way of life, and not go down tryin' to fight off both the Yankees and them slave owners—weuns never had no truck with either one."

Charlie came in just then, with a gunnysack over his shoulder; the boy left it on the table and went out again. His grandfather opened the sack, revealing a good-sized haunch of venison. He produced a butcher knife and began to work on it.

Intrigued by the story he was hearing— seeing it as a way to satisfy his curiosity about these Cagles of Missouri Gulch—Jim Bannister prompted the other man: "So the whole clan of you picked up and moved here to Colorado?"

"Wa'n't no trick. Was fewer of us Cagles then, and all in the habit of lookin' to me as the head, to make decisions. Things is changed some now, of course. Today they's about a dozen families strung along the creek, and the young ones have growed and some are gettin' restless. They say they want to up and leave."

The old man shook his head; his eyes seemed troubled as they followed the work the veined and wrinkled hands were doing on the red meat, with skilled strokes of the blade. "Well, I can see their thinkin'. I was a sprout myself, once, like Vern and Dewey and them. I can understand ours don't seem too easy a life, once they get notions of what it would be outside. The winters, for one thing, are sure as hell worse than they was, back where weuns come from. But, in time you get used to that.

"Far's I'm concerned, hit's been a good life. We got all that's really needful, and these years we've kept safe and out of mischief. Besides, we all taken the oath and now we got to stick by it; at least, that's what *I* say. Trouble is, nobody seems to pay mind to what I think anymore. Brother Martin is running things, here in the gulch— wa'n't for Charlie gettin' around and actin' as my eyes and ears, likely I'd never know nothin' of what goes on. Seems I'm just old Phin Cagle, that nobody needs to bother about . . ."

He had been busy all the time he talked, sawing at the meat. Now he stuck the knife point into the tabletop and declared, "That ought to give you a few meals, anyway, till you're where you can pick up more. I can throw in a little salt and some Arbuckle's, to tide you over."

"You're more than generous," Bannister said, well aware that food staples, that had to be packed in here over the terrible trail from outside, must always be in short supply. But one remark of Phin Cagle's had caught at his attention and he asked, curiously, "What was it you said a moment ago? Something about taking an oath—"

There was an interruption as the boy, Charlie, popped in through the door, gesturing wildly and with excitement written on his face. Charlie seemed to have a cleft palate; it was hard to make out the hollow and unformed speech that spilled from him, but Bannister thought he distinguished one word: "Rider!" In almost the same instant he heard the growing sound of hoof-beats.

From the boy's manner, whoever was approaching couldn't be anyone he knew—not a member of the Cagle clan; it must be another stranger. Phin Cagle was already hobbling outside, behind his grandson. Quickly Bannister was on his feet and as far as the door. There, standing back just out of sight, he watched Wes Dodd pulling rein before the cabin.

Bannister's cheek muscles tightened and his hand closed on the butt of the holstered gun. The newcomer's face was without expression as he looked from one to the other of the Cagles. He had no weapon showing, but Bannister didn't doubt he'd have replaced the one lost from that clip holster under his coat. He held himself stiffly, as though he might be hurting from the clubbing blow to the chest Bannister had dealt him with the empty shotgun.

The reins loose in his hands, the manhunter gave Phin Cagle a brief nod which the latter wordlessly returned. Two strangers, in one day— it was probably enough to startle the garrulous old man into silence. Now Wes Dodd turned and looked at the dun that stood under saddle and gear, tied to the corral fence. The manhunter was smoking one of his cigars. He took it from his mouth and pointed with it.

"I know this animal," he said. "I happen to be looking for the owner. You wouldn't happen to know where he is?"

Phin Cagle took his time about answering; Bannister, watching from the shadows inside the door, had a sudden intuition the old man was reluctant to betray a guest—even a stranger about whom he knew nothing. When he did answer, it was with a question of his own: "This feller you're lookin' for: Could you say what he looks like?"

"He's easy enough to spot," Dodd replied coolly. "A big fellow, bigger than most you'll see—towheaded, with the beginning of a beard. And since he lost his horse, he'd be afoot . . ."

At that point, Jim Bannister decided the thing had gone far enough. Phin Cagle, and his slow-witted grandson, were both utterly harmless and without defense; he could no longer bring himself to stay hidden and let the old man bear the brunt of Wes Dodd's suspicious questioning. Deliberately he stepped out the door, into the sun.

"Hello, Dodd," he said calmly. "I guess you found me."

His enemy's head swung sharply; aside from that Dodd gave no sign of what emotion lay behind the jet-black stare. He deliberately replaced the cigar between his lips before he said, around it, "You had me guessing. Just what are you doing here?"

"Collecting my horse," Bannister answered. "These good people found him running loose, and I happened to spot him in their corral."

"That was lucky." Dodd looked again at the old man, and at Charlie who was standing slack-jawed. He nodded curtly. "Very lucky," he repeated, and to Phin Cagle he said, "I'm sure my partner's grateful."

The old man blinked. "Partner?" He looked surprised, and then a little hurt. "You never mentioned you had a partner," he told Bannister accusingly.

Bannister shrugged. "I guess I didn't, did I?"

Wes Dodd had grown suddenly impatient. He jerked his narrow head at Bannister. "You better get mounted. We got distance to cover and the day's pretty well used . . . Well?" he added, his voice sharpening when Bannister made no move and no answer. "Are you coming?"

Bannister stood there with the sunlight warm on his bare head, causing him to squint a little as he slanted a look at the man on the roan. What finally decided him was a reluctance about involving the old man and his slow-witted grandson in unnecessary trouble. With a shrug he broke from where he stood and walked out to his waiting horse; but Wes Dodd surely knew that the showdown was only being postponed.

Phin Cagle said suddenly, "I damn near forgot! Hold on, while I fetch that grub." He turned and went back in the cabin for it.

At one side Charlie watched with his habitual dull expression. In that moment no one was close enough to overhear as Wes Dodd leaned near, saying quietly, "Here's something should keep you from making any mistakes, friend Bannister." And he opened the hand he had dipped into a pocket of his corduroy coat. Bannister, standing beside his horse holding the reins, looked and felt a cold chill as he recognized the tiny object lying on the other's palm.

It was a gold-mounted jade earring.

CHAPTER XII

For all her attempt at bravery, Stella Harbord had scarcely seen Jim Bannister disappear into the rocks and timber below their hiding place when she was overwhelmed by a desolating sense of aloneness and danger. Suddenly it was all she could do to keep from bursting into futile tears. She lectured herself out of that, but a lethargy of dull shock remained; her ankle pained her, and though the warm sun concentrated among the rock faces helped to dry her clothing, there was still the memory of icy water closing over her head.

To keep herself occupied she busied her hands with taking down her hair, combing it out as best she could with her fingers and spreading it over her shoulders to dry. After that she could only huddle in her place, listening to the voice of the rushing creek and the stillness that magnified her own appalling isolation, and her deepening anxiety over Jim Bannister. She thought of the risks he might even now be taking, of the trouble he'd undergone because of her—leading his enemies to him, making herself a burden, and now hurting her ankle so that they could go no farther at all until he had somehow found a horse for her.

It had all been an unbroken litany of disaster, and she could only blame herself.

Surely, hours must have passed; yet reason told her the angle of the sun, and the lay of shadows cast by the boulders around her, had barely shifted—her own anxieties, and nothing else, were stretching each dragging moment and packing it with agonies of suspense . . . Suddenly, then, under the masking noise of the creek she became aware of a horseman slowly approaching.

For an instant she thought it must be Jim Bannister returning already, and she started to her feet despite a pang of agony from the swollen ankle. Just in time the truth struck home. That rider was coming from the north—exactly the wrong direction! He seemed to be following the creekbank, at a walk; as she crouched listening to the measured strike of shod hoofs draw nearer, Stella Harbord found herself shaking and all at once scarcely able to breathe.

Something told her this was one of the men who'd followed the hounds upcreek, hunting them; realizing the trail was lost, he could have crossed to search the near bank for it—his slow, deliberate rate of travel suggested that was precisely what he must be doing. The listening and waiting became hardly bearable. By now she judged he must have come even with the nest of boulders, and feeling an ache in her palms she looked down to discover her fists were clenched so tight the nails had dug deep. She forced her hands open, spread them on her thighs to stop their trembling.

The rider halted. For a long moment after that there was nothing at all—the silence seemed almost to scream along her nerves as she pictured the rider, whoever he was, halted to study the marks of Jim Bannister's boots in the mud, then lifting his glance to follow their course.

Then the horse was in motion again, and this time she could tell it was coming up the slight incline of the bank, straight in her direction.

She fought to her feet, one steadying hand against the sun-warmed surface of a boulder, and looked desperately about. A hundred feet away were the nearest trees—if she stayed low, she just might be able to keep the boulders between her and the horseman long enough to get that far unnoticed.

On the desperate hope, she started for them. The damaged ankle betrayed her. She managed to use it, despite the stabbing agony that every step cost her; but when she had covered something less than half the distance, loose rubble turned underfoot. She lost her balance and went down, crying out sharply. On hands and knees, helpless, she heard a shout and the rider was spurring toward her. He reined in his horse, iron shoes plowing up loose grit to shower her; she stared dully for a moment at a skittish pair of black-stockinged forelegs. She raised her head, then, and her glance moved to the horse's muscled shoulder—black hide gleaming faintly with sweat—and then on up the rider's slab-like shape until it met the pale eyes of Dewey Cagle, peering down at her.

"Well, well!" he said in his nasal Missouri twang. "Would you just look what we got here!"

For a moment she thought she might faint, from pain and terror. Dewey turned for a look around him; when he failed to see what he was searching for he demanded harshly, "All right—where is he? Where's Jim Bannister?"

So by now the hillbillies had learned the real identity of the man they were hunting—and probably, also, the amount of the price on his head. She could imagine what a fantastic sum it must appear to the likes of them, and the lengths they might go to lay hands on it. Somehow this news made the situation seem all the more hopeless, and her heart sank.

Irritated by her silence, Dewey Cagle scowled and now he swung out of the saddle, to stand directly over her. "I ast you a question," he reminded her, and when he still got no answer he leaned and grabbed her by an arm and hauled her up. His sweating face only inches from her own, he repeated: "Where'd Bannister go to?"

Stella shook her head numbly. "I don't know...."

The beard-stubbled lips twisted. "Pulled out

and left you, did he? Savin' his own hide!" The man shook his head. "Now, why should a good-lookin' female waste time on somebody like that?"

Holding her, he eyed her speculatively. Stella knew he was looking at her breasts; for a dreadful moment she could see the idea of rape reflected plainly in his narrow eyes. But warring impulses seemed to be at work, inhibiting him. The gleam in his eye turned dull, and he said roughly, "I think you better come along, and let Vern and Mr. Dodd figure whut to do about you. Let's go!"

She had to clutch at him to keep from fainting with pain, when she put her weight on the injured ankle. Impatient, Dewey Cagle caught her above the hips with both his big hands and all but threw her into the saddle. A moment later he swung up behind her; she smelled the stale sweat on his clothing, as his kick sent the black leaping ahead and Stella was thrown hard against him.

They rode in silence. There were many things Stella would have liked to know, but she was terribly afraid of this man and she could not bring herself to make conversation, not with his big, dirty hand clasping her middle and his breath hot against her cheek. Since the only distance she could create between them was silence, she held her tongue. Dewey Cagle, on his part, must have been under some pressures, for he kept the black horse moving as though he were anxious to get wherever they were going. And he spoke no more than she.

As it turned out, they didn't have far to travel. Their destination proved to be yet another of the rude log cabins that seemed to dot the whole length of this gulch; this was perhaps one of the oldest. It sat on an open flat quite near the creek, whose current churned and boiled here over a massive rock shoulder and threw up a mist that, through the years, had turned one end of the cabin roof bright green with moss.

Behind a fringe of trees the canyon wall rose quite close, and somehow it looked familiar. All at once Stella knew why: It was the identical section she and Jim Bannister had studied from a distance, thinking they saw indications of a trail. Now, from this angle, she couldn't say for certain whether they had been right or not.

Dewey rode up to a halt, slid off the black's rump. He made a quick tie, anchoring the reins to an iron ring sunk into a log of the cabin's side wall, and then looked at Stella who had remained motionless in the saddle. "All right," he grunted. "Git down."

She found when she dismounted that she could just barely trust her weight to the injured ankle. Dewey Cagle still seemed unaware or indifferent to her hurt; impatient, he grabbed her arm to hustle her inside, batting the door open and all but hurling her across the low slab threshold. She caught the edge of the jamb to steady herself as she blinked against the dark interior.

There were only two people in the room. The first her glance lit on was Wes Dodd. The manhunter sat at a slab table with a jug in front of him, and a tin cup that looked as though it held some of the Cagles' home-distilled whiskey. His shirt and coat had been removed and hung over the back of his chair, and his naked torso was swathed in tight bandages—she thought, with grim satisfaction, that must be evidence of the blow with the shotgun that knocked him off his horse.

He was just picking up his drink, but when he saw the newcomers in the doorway he set the cup down hard and gave Stella a long scrutiny, so cold and filled with venom that she shuddered. Something in his eyes told her how she must look to him—dirty and bedraggled, her traveling dress reduced to a ruin, her hands and face scratched and bleeding where tree branches and sharp stones had broken the skin.

Dodd lifted a stabbing glance to the man who stood beside her. "What about Bannister?"

"The woman's all I found," Dewey told him. "I *knowed* Cousin Vern was wrong to keep lookin' upstream. I tried the other direction, and sure enough I spotted where they clumb out—pretty close to the place weuns lost the trail. And there she was, hidin' in the rocks—all alone. No Bannister."

"And no tracks?" the other demanded sharply.

"I never looked for none," Dewey Cagle admitted. "I couldn't, not with her on my hands. Anyway I figured you'd be wantin' to know, right off, what I'd found. He ain't likely goin' to get far."

Dodd scowled and drummed his fingers on the table. And now, from the place where she stood behind his chair, the cabin's other occupant suddenly spoke up. "The poor thing looks plumb tuckered. You ain't gonna make her stand in that doorway all afternoon?"

Stella had taken her for a child, until she spoke; apparently the girl was older than that, but not really much more—sixteen or seventeen, perhaps, with immature breasts and narrow hips inside a dress that looked rather too small for her. Though she spoke to Dewey, she only looked at him out of the corners of her eyes; you might have thought she was cringing away from a possible blow. Young as she was, Stella thought this girl had the air of someone whom life had cowed and permanently frightened.

"Just look sharp, that's all!" Dewey said gruffly. "Give her half a chance and she'll run. Cain't take your eyes off her a minute." But he released his prisoner's arm and gave her a shove into the room.

The two women exchanged a long look. It was the first real spark of sympathy Stella had received and she warmed to it, even from a waif of a mountain girl. Her arms and legs were thin, her feet bare and dirty. She had her hair tied back with a bit of ribbon, as though in an attempt to add a touch of prettiness to her sallow face.

The gauntness of her cheeks made her eyes look big and brown and timid as a faun's. She asked diffidently, "Could you use something to eat, maybe?"

The mere mention of food was almost enough to make Stella's knees cave with weakness. "Oh, yes!" she exclaimed. "If it would be possible. But, I wonder—could I clean up a little, first?"

"Why, you sure can!" But as Stella started forward, the girl seemed to notice what the others had missed. "You're a-limpin'! You been hurt?" And at Stella's nod, she took her arm and led her to the table. "Lady, you set right here. I'll fetch soap and water."

"Thank you . . ."

Stella let herself down onto one of the crudely fashioned chairs; Dewey Cagle repeated his dark warning: "You heard what I said, Linda Fay. She hain't to be trusted!"

The girl shot him one of her frightened looks. "Yes, Dewey." But she hurried off to the fireplace.

Meanwhile Wes Dodd had got to his feet and was pulling on his shirt, over the bandages. He moved gingerly and Dewey Cagle, watching his face, asked, "How you feeling now, Mr. Dodd?"

"Ready to go again," the manhunter said shortly as he worked at the buttons. "I thought the bastard might have done real damage to a couple of my ribs, but it seems otherwise. And your wife's done a good job with the bandaging." He nodded to Linda Fay, who was coming back to the table with a steaming tin washbasin, a bar of yellow homemade soap.

So the girl was married to Dewey Cagle, Stella thought, and wondered whether she had come here to the gulch from outside. More likely she was a cousin—she had some of the Cagle look herself. How many of her husband's relatives crowded in with them, in this littered cabin? The walls were lined with bunks, and one end of the single room had been curtained as though in a crude attempt at privacy.

Stella was aware now of the men watching her; resolutely ignoring them, she opened the collar of her torn and filthy blouse, pushed up her sleeves. The towel was rough and the soap as strong as lye, but when she dipped a corner of the cloth into the steaming water, and gratefully touched it to her face, she had no complaint—she was too grateful for a chance to get half-way clean again, to feel half-way human.

Linda Fay suggested, "Later, weuns can rench that ankle. Nothin' like a good hot soakin' to take the swelling out."

Stella thanked her with a nod.

Shirt buttoned, Wes Dodd took up his gun-harness and slipped into it, strapped the filled holster into place beneath his left arm—Stella wondered if the gun was a mate to the one Jim Bannister took from him. He was very particular about the fit of the harness and the seating of the weapon. Finally satisfied, he reached for his corduroy coat and shrugged into it. He asked Dewey Cagle, "If Bannister set out to try and locate horses for himself and the woman, where would be the likeliest place?"

The younger man screwed up his face, considering. "Headed downstream, this side the creek, first he'd come to would be old Phin's. Phin has him a couple of broncs."

"That's the one you told me about? Used to be the head man in this family?"

"Yeah, but nobody pays him any mind nowadays—some of us figure he's gettin' kind of simple. Charlie, that lives with him, ain't too bright either."

"Doesn't sound as though they'd give much trouble to anyone as desperate as Bannister."

Dewey wagged his bony head. "Prob'ly not, for a fact."

"Then," Wes Dodd said crisply as he took his

171

hat from the floor beside his chair, "I'd better move fast!"

Stella saw the look on his face, and what it promised for Jim Bannister so overwhelmed her that her heart sank. She didn't even hear what Linda Fay said to her; the girl had to repeat it: "Them's the prettiest things . . ."

"What?" she said absently.

"Them," Linda Fay said, and timidly touched a finger to one of the earrings that had been revealed when she pushed the hair back across her shoulders.

Stella managed a smile. "Thank you—I like them too. They're jade. They were a present from—" Jim Bannister's name died on her tongue as she saw Wes Dodd looking at her with a sharper interest.

He held out a hand. "Let me see one of those." When she only returned the look, his voice turned quickly hard. "Are you going to take that thing out of your ear and give it to me? Or do I tear it out?"

Convinced he would actually do it, she hastily dried her hands on the towel and, with numbed fingers, undid the fastening and placed the object in his hand. She watched his face as he examined it, letting it catch the light. Abruptly he nodded, dropped the earring into a pocket of his coat; he said crisply, "If friend Bannister sees this, he'll understand what it means!" And, turning

172

to Dewey Cagle: "My horse—is it still saddled?"

"In the corral." As he saw the other start for the door the young fellow added quickly, "You want me along, don't you?"

Dodd shook his head. "Until your cousin Vern gets back, I want you here. The woman's your responsibility. While we've got her, Jim Bannister is as good as ours. I'm charging you to see that nothing spoils it."

"Nothin' will," Dewey promised. Wes Dodd was dragging on his hat as he strode outside, moving stiffly to favor his bandaged ribs.

CHAPTER XIII

There was a flash of brightness and Bannister caught the earring Wes Dodd tossed him. His face felt like a bleak mask; Dodd read his expression and nodded. "She hasn't been hurt," he said. "In case you're wondering."

Through set lips Bannister promised him, "If I find that she has—!"

"No point in threatening me," the other said calmly. "Barring a sore ankle, she was in good enough shape when I left her. If you have hope of seeing her again, you know what you have to do."

His meaning could not have been any clearer. In that moment pure hatred lay bare in the look that passed between the two of them. And now Phin Cagle came from the shack, carrying a gunnysack, and the tense moment broke as Bannister turned to accept it. "I thrun in some cold flapjacks," the old man told him. "Should be grub enough to see you and your partner quite a piece."

Bannister accepted it with thanks that were genuine. As he lashed the bag behind his saddle, old Phin warned him, "Careful as you go—try not to run into more of my kin than you have to. Some can git mighty mean, where strangers is concerned."

"Thanks for the reminder." Jim Bannister was acutely aware of Wes Dodd listening, watchful and tense at every word that passed between them; but he had no intention of saying anything that might involve this gentle old man in danger. He found the stirrup, swung into saddle. Wes Dodd lifted the reins; Bannister booted the dun to put him alongside the manhunter's animal. He nodded to the old man, and they rode away stirrup to stirrup—exactly as though they were, in fact, the saddle partners Dodd had labeled them for Phin Cagle's benefit.

As they rode, Bannister narrowly watched the other, and once he caught a fleeting grimace of pain as the roan made a misstep. He said, dryly, "You don't look real comfortable."

Dodd shot him a hard glance. "I'm still not sure you didn't splinter a rib for me."

"Believe me, I'd have hit you harder except that that shotgun went to pieces on me."

The manhunter's jaw muscles bunched but he made no answer to that. As they rode on, Phin Cagle's cabin gradually fell from sight behind them; in good time they skirted a slight hump of land and their way dropped toward the creek. Here, alone with the busy murmur of the water and no other eyes to observe them, they halted their mounts and swung to face each other.

"So, we meet again," Jim Bannister said crisply. "Now what?"

As the manhunter met his look, the roan horse he was riding sidestepped; again, Dodd winced slightly and started a hand toward the gap in his coat, as though to touch the hurting rib. Bannister, remembering the shoulder holster, quickly shook his head. "Don't do that!" He dropped his own hand to rest on his gunbelt. His enemy scowled, but withdrew the hand and laid it on the pommel of his saddle.

Bannister went on, "I'm to turn myself over to you, I suppose? And what happens to the woman?"

"That's up to you," Wes Dodd answered. "Depends on whether you care enough for her safety, that you'll pledge yourself to give me no trouble. For openers, let's say you hand over the gun you took from me."

Bannister shook his head. "I think we'll just leave things like they are, for now. All right?"

"A standoff?" the manhunter said sharply.

"Or an armed truce."

The other seemed to lose some of the hold on his temper. "Maybe you've forgotten I have the whip hand!" Wes Dodd snapped. "Your woman is in the hands right now of men who are little better than animals. Do I have to spell out for you what could happen?"

It took all Bannister's control to keep his voice steady. "I haven't forgotten anything—including the fact that I'm worth no more to you alive than dead. I might as well put a bullet through my own head, as surrender my gun and expect you to honor any bargains!"

The jet-black eyes bored into him. "Keep the gun, then, damn you. But believe me—I can kill you if you try to use it!"

Bannister didn't doubt the other had reason for confidence in his ability to use the weapon he carried under his coat; but all he said was, "Maybe . . ." With the point settled, Wes Dodd gave a jerk at the reins and swung his horse around. Each man kept a wary attention on the other as they headed north, back along the trail that had brought both of them to Phin Cagle's cabin.

Leaf shadows slid across them; to their left the creek kept up its busy clamor, as the horses' hoofs rang from rock surfaces or made sucking sounds in gumbo left by last night's rain. Jim Bannister, tormented by fears for Stella, rode in a black fog of mounting concern. He was about to demand a faster pace when Wes Dodd said suddenly, "We can cross here."

Bannister pulled up sharply. He looked for recent horse tracks where the level bank shelved away toward sun-struck water, and finding none he put a searching stare on the manhunter. "Cross the creek?" he repeated. "Why?"

"You want me to take you to your woman, don't you—by the shortest route?"

"I don't trust you a minute," Bannister said flatly. "I'm sure you've been figuring how to do those Cagles out of any deal you may have made with them. Nothing would suit you better than to manage some way to sneak me out of the gulch and away from here, and leave them Stella Harbord."

His only clue that he had guessed right showed in the slightest change of expression flickering across that other, dark face. Jim Bannister's controls nearly snapped as he saw it. The nails of one fist ground into the palm. "Forget it, Dodd! Rather than let you sidetrack me, I'll start at the place where I left her and read the signs for myself. Because I don't intend to be fooled—not with her at stake!"

A long moment, the words seemed to hang between them. Then Wes Dodd shrugged and turned away, lifting the reins.

Bannister, satisfied with having made his point, was almost taken by surprise. A sudden kick of Dodd's boot against its flank startled the roan, so that the ugly brute snorted and leaped sideward, slamming full into the dun. Bannister could have been unseated as his animal floundered briefly in the slick mud. A wrench of his wrist helped steady the horse, while at the same moment he made a hurried grab for the gun in his holster. But Dodd was crowding him, trapping his arm and preventing him from clearing the weapon, even as the manhunter dug for the one in his own shoulder harness. Bannister glimpsed it in his hand, sliding into the open.

There was only one option, and Jim Bannister took it. He lifted his right arm, elbow bent, and with all his force drove it into the other man. He was trying for a damaged rib, and the answering shout of pain told him he had connected. Dodd reeled away, and Bannister pawed at his holster while he was still trying with the reins to get the dun settled. After that, the gun was in his fingers, and he saw Wes Dodd doubled forward with an arm clamped about his middle. Dodd had dropped his gun into the mud and it looked as though he might slide out of the saddle and follow it down.

Bannister had to dismount and grab the roan's headstall to steady it. A shudder ran through Wes Dodd and when he lifted his face it looked almost gray, but there was pure hatred in the glare he turned on Bannister. His mouth twisted and he swore, tightly and wickedly.

The other met his look with no trace of sympathy. "I can fight dirty, too," Bannister pointed out. "You're only lucky I'm not the killer the syndicate says—because when I think what you're doing to Stella Harbord, I could be tempted."

His enemy looked at the gun, eyes bright with pain. "Kill me," he said harshly, "and you lose your only chance of seeing her alive!"

"Maybe, and maybe not. The fact remains, I'm no killer—but it wouldn't be smart right now to tempt me. . . ."

He located the weapon the prisoner had dropped; to his surprise it proved to be his own sixshooter. With plenty of ammunition in the loops of his shell belt, he once more felt equipped to give a fight. He dropped the gun into its holster, shoving Wes Dodd's gun behind his belt. He swung up again into the saddle and looked at the other man.

"All right," he said. "The situation seems to have changed a little. We'll go on now."

Wes Dodd was probably not hurt too seriously—the face he showed Bannister was mottled as much with fury as with pain. Ordered to move out, he merely glared defiantly; so Jim Bannister simply gave the roan a stinging swipe with his rein ends. The animal lunged ahead and he sent the dun after it.

As he rode, Bannister dug into the gunnysack lashed behind his saddle and brought out a couple of Phin Cagle's cold flapjacks; munching on these helped, for now, to blunt the worst edge of his hunger—he could hope later for a chance to do something with that generous chunk of venison.

Now, having arrived at the place where he left Stella, he took time to study the tracks and piece out part of the drama that had happened here. It wasn't hard to pick up sign of a single horseman approaching the boulders, of Stella's attempt to flee and being run down and captured where she fell. A knot of brute anger formed in him as he read the story; he found Wes Dodd staring at him and wondered at what might be showing in his face. "Was it you?" he demanded harshly.

The other lifted a shoulder within the corduroy coat. "Me? No, as a matter of fact it was Dewey found her and brought her in. Not that I can see it makes any difference."

"No difference at all," Bannister agreed bleakly. "I'd expect almost anything from an ignorant set of hillbillies like the Cagles. But *you,* friend—I promise you, if they've hurt her it's you I'll be settling with. Be thinking about that!"

He didn't need to elaborate.

If Dodd had ideas of throwing him off, Dewey Cagle's plain trail settled that: it was too clear to be missed. When the cabin itself at last came in sight, with smoke rising from the chimney to indicate someone was there, the sign led straight toward it. He knew at once this had to be the place.

It stood some hundred yards ahead of them, near the bank where the creek tossed up a constant churning spray. They came on it without warning, and Wes Dodd had already ridden into the open before Bannister could think to stop him. Too late, swearing at the loss of any chance for surprise, Jim Bannister hauled on the rein.

Only for a moment. If the Cagles were watching from behind those blank, dark windows, they'd have the manhunter spotted by this time. Bannister realized he could neither order him back without rousing suspicion, nor let him ride on alone; so without any choice he kicked the dun and sent it forward. But as he drew alongside the other, he let Dodd see the gun he had drawn and held, inconspicuously, in his lap.

"Just keep riding easy," he warned. "And look natural."

"You planning to ride up and announce yourself?"

Bannister didn't bother to answer, and Wes Dodd obeyed without argument. Drawing nearer, keeping pace with the roan, Bannister fought a mounting tightness as he studied the silent cabin and the corral that held a pair of horses. If guns were covering him, he could only hope their owners were satisfied that the jade earring had done its work, that he was coming in with Wes Dodd to surrender himself in trade for Stella. What happened next, when he got within short-gun range, was something else again. . . .

There was a flicker of movement to his right; Bannister looked and there was Dewey Cagle, stepping out of the trees with a rifle in his hands.

"You got him, Mr. Dodd!" he shouted excitedly. "By God, you done it—you brung him in!"

He was cut off by Wes Dodd's frantic yell. "*Shoot him!* Don't stand there, you idiot! Kill him dead . . ." In the same instant Dodd was sawing with the reins, trying to get out of the line of fire. Bannister barely had time to throw himself forward along the dun's neck as the rifle spoke.

The bullet came close enough that he felt the tap of displaced air. Dewey Cagle was standing spread-legged, frantically working the lever for a second try, when Bannister managed to bring his sixshooter up. With the dun moving under him and endangering his aim, he flung off a hurried shot that mingled with the echoes of the rifle. He didn't really count on making a hit; he could scarcely believe it when he saw the other man knocked spinning off his feet, losing the rifle as he went down.

From the way he fell Bannister thought he would stay down. There wasn't time to spare Dewey a closer look. Settling the dun, he glanced quickly about and discovered Wes Dodd heading for the trees. But the manhunter had seen Cagle drop, and now as the muzzle of the smoking gun turned on him he apparently decided he couldn't outrun a bullet. When Bannister yelled at him Wes Dodd pulled rein and turned back, scowling.

Bannister's own nerves were vibrating with

tension as he remembered Vern Cagle was still to be accounted for. At any second he half expected another gun to open up on him. But those two shots had battered themselves to silence against the granite wall that lifted above the gulch at this point, and now an uneasy quiet had settled, to be broken only by the busy clamor of the creek. Bannister drew a long breath, and with his gunbarrel motioned Wes Dodd ahead of him toward the cabin.

CHAPTER XIV

Someone was in the doorway—not Vern but a woman, who looked scarcely more than a child as she stood barefooted, staring, with both hands pressed against her mouth. Now she broke and darted past Bannister's horse, bare legs flashing as she went at a run toward the place where Dewey Cagle lay sprawled.

Bannister thought of the rifle the man had flung away as he fell, but forgot it when he heard Stella say his name. She stepped from the doorway, hobbling a little but apparently able to use the hurt ankle. Her expression mingled relief, fright, and joy at the sight of him. At once he booted the dun and when he reined in and reached a hand down to her she caught it in both of hers. She seemed beyond speech.

"They haven't hurt you?" he demanded.

She shook her head quickly. "No—no!" In fact, she looked fine, except for the signs of strain and deep concern. She had done something with her hair, and though her clothing was torn and bedraggled she'd managed to wash the grime and traces of dried blood from her face and hands.

"What about Vern Cagle?" he demanded, because that was a threat never far from his thoughts.

"He isn't here. When they gave up and sent the dogs home, he continued up the creek alone— he was sure he could cut our trail. Dewey rode downstream, and he was the one who found me . . . Oh, Jim!" she went on, clutching his hand as though she could never let it go. "I've died a thousand times, this past hour. I wasn't worried so much about myself, as what they might have been able to make *you* do . . ."

"Because of this?" He took from his pocket the jade earring that matched the one she still wore, and handed it down to her. "I'll admit I had some bad moments, when I saw him holding it. I told him . . . if anything happened to you—" He didn't finish the speech, but let his look settle on the prisoner.

Wes Dodd had his share of calm control. He returned Bannister's stare, and even with a gun pointed at him nothing showed in his narrow and impassive features. "What are you going to do about him?" Stella asked.

Bannister had been wondering about that himself. Now, glancing around he saw an answer. To his prisoner he said curtly, "Get down."

Wes Dodd seemed to be trying to read the look in Bannister's eyes, but not succeeding; under the muzzle of the gun, he swung a leg across the saddle and stepped unhurriedly to the ground. Suddenly there was the first flicker of alarm as he saw what Bannister had removed from somewhere in his clothing. Dodd's head jerked and he backed away a step. "No!" The exclamation burst from him.

But Jim Bannister was already kicking the dun forward, crowding the other man; before Wes Dodd could leap clear he leaned and, with a flash of metal and a sharp click, one of the pair of handcuffs snapped on Dodd's left wrist. After that, Bannister gave his horse the boot, and the manhunter, shouting and struggling now, was being dragged toward the corner of the shack where an iron hitching ring was kept shiny by the horses' reins that had been tethered to it. Another quick movement, and the manhunter was firmly shackled there. Bannister tested the ring, satisfied himself that it was securely sunk into the wood. He nodded and said "That should hold you. I had an idea those things would come in handy, if I hung onto them."

It was nearly the first time he had seen any breach in the man's cool surface. Dodd had lost his hat and there was sweat on his face; he flashed a hatefilled look at Bannister through the hair that had fallen across his eyes. "It's not finished!" he said harshly. "Before it is, you'll be wearing these again!"

"Think so?" Bannister looked down at his own sore and badly chafed wrists. He thought of the ordeal he and Stella had been put through, and suddenly real anger took hold of him. "We'll

187

see about that!" he said suddenly, with such vehemence that the prisoner recoiled as he saw Bannister's hand start toward his hip.

But he didn't draw the gun. Instead, he dug into a pocket and then he was turning and standing in the stirrups, as his arm made an arc above his head. A bit of metal streaked brightly and was gone; looking again at Wes Dodd he said grimly, "That, my friend, was the key. Maybe somebody can fish it out of the creek for you, if you're lucky; if not, you can wear those things yourself for awhile. But I don't think you'll be putting them on anyone else!"

Wes Dodd began to curse him, in a monotonous litany of foul language, but Bannister was no longer listening. Turning to Stella, he said, "Let's get out of here."

She hesitated. "What about her?" And she indicated where the girl from the cabin had gone down on her knees beside Dewey Cagle's motionless body.

"Who is she?"

"Her name is Linda Fay. She's Dewey's wife—though she's hardly more than a child. She was very kind. She fed me, and soaked and bandaged my ankle. I feel bad just to go off and—"

"Wait here." He turned and rode the short distance, to dismount beside the girl and the man he had shot.

Dewey's rifle still lay where it had been

dropped; she apparently wasn't interested in it. Instead she had opened her husband's jacket and shirt to expose the shoulder wound Bannister's lead had given him, and was using a piece torn from his shirt to stanch the flow of blood. She looked up. Her cheeks were shining with tears, her eyes solemn but unaccusing as they met his.

Dewey Cagle wasn't much but she seemed genuinely concerned about him. Something constrained Bannister to tell her, "I'm sorry, Linda Fay. I wouldn't have shot him if he hadn't shot first. But a man has to protect himself." She offered no reply to that. He went down beside her to make his own estimate of the wound's seriousness. "A clean hole. He's tough and he's young; he'll mend . . . Let me help you get him to the house."

The young fellow was all bone and solid muscle, wiry and spare; it was not too difficult to handle him. He roused a little, groaning, as Bannister lifted him and got a shoulder beneath the uninjured arm. "Bring my horse," Bannister told the girl. After that he half walked, half carried the hurt man to the cabin, past Wes Dodd who scowled murderously from where he stood shackled to the wall.

Inside, Bannister eased the hurt man onto a chair by the table and then Linda Fay, having left the dun on anchoring reins, was hurrying to take over. He stood to watch her a moment;

189

she seemed completely competent and no longer even aware of him, and after a moment he turned away. As he did he saw a hat on a wall peg that looked familiar. Sure enough, it was his own, lost that morning on the creekbank. He took it and pulled it on, and waited by the door for Stella, who was talking to Linda Fay. She was offering the hillbilly girl the jade earrings.

"You liked these," she said. "I'd be pleased for you to have them."

Linda Fay looked at the trinkets lying in Stella's palm, but she hastily shook her head and stepped back, putting both hands behind her. "Oh, no ma'am!" she exclaimed. "I couldn't take your purties."

"I do wish you would. I can't pay you for your kindness."

But she doggedly refused. "Twa'n't nothing. Anyhow—*they* wouldn't let me keep 'em, was they to find out."

Stella gave it up. "All right, Linda Fay," she said. "I'm glad your husband wasn't hurt too badly. I'm sure he'll be all right." And she turned away from the girl's blue eyes, which were something like a frightened and half-wild creature's, and—still limping—rejoined Bannister in the doorway.

Feeling keenly the need to get away from there, Bannister lost no more time helping Stella onto the dun's saddle and adjusting the stirrups for her. He knew she could manage that horse, whereas the hammerheaded roan was an unknown quantity. Wes Dodd watched in sullen silence until he saw Bannister gathering the roan's ground-anchored leathers; that stung a cry from him: "So now you're stealing my horse, damn you!"

"It's not your horse," Stella reminded him. "I heard Dewey Cagle joke about scaring it out of the station man at Ute Springs."

"In that case," Bannister said as he swung up to the other saddle, "it's hardly stealing, is it? I'll do you a favor, Dodd—I'll try to see the roan gets back to its owner, and relieve you of the worry."

Wes Dodd swore at him again. Ignoring him, Bannister nodded to Stella and led the way out of the dooryard.

At some distance, hearing a shout, they looked back. Linda Fay had appeared in the door to watch them go; and now they heard Dodd yelling at her: "Damn it, woman! Find me a crowbar—something to pry me loose . . ." She didn't look at him or even seem to hear. A moment later she turned back inside and firmly closed the slab door behind her, leaving Wes Dodd futilely struggling with the shackles that held him anchored.

The roan was tough-jawed but a firm rein could manage it. With a horse for each of them, his own gun in his holster, and even—thanks to old

Phin Cagle—a supply of food, Jim Bannister felt for once that the odds were no longer stacked against them. Still, there could be no easing of the pressures until they had somehow found a way out of this gulch. He knew Stella Harbord was bursting with questions, anxious to learn just how he'd managed to beat Wes Dodd and regain the dun, but this was not the moment.

From earliest morning their one aim had been to achieve the trail Bannister spotted leading up the north wall of the gulch; now it was within reach and on one accord they turned toward it. A horse track led that way, threading for a quarter of a mile or so through brush and timber that grew behind the cabin. Where the growth fell back, the ground began abruptly to lift and the trail went up in switchbacks, across nearly naked rock. It looked like a second cousin of the one they had followed here from Ute Springs—narrow, steep, but well marked with travel.

"When I had a chance," Stella said, "I tried to get Linda Fay to tell me if this trail would take us out of the gulch. She didn't answer—only looked at me, in the strangest way. I didn't know what to make of it . . ."

Neither did Bannister, but after a moment's hesitation he shrugged. "As we said about the one last night—a trail has to go somewhere. If there's any chance of getting out this way, I'd prefer to check it out before deciding we have to try going back the way we came, and facing all that again."

"I would, too," she said. Bannister took the lead, and they started up.

It wasn't really as precipitous as it looked, but once they had climbed above the tree level they had some spectacular views of the gulch—almost like a hatchet slash, chopped deep into the flank of the mountains. When he looked at it, and at the tumbling white water of the creek at its heart, Bannister wondered a little how they had ever found a way through, on foot and traveling blind. While they halted once, to talk and rest the horses, he transferred Dodd's captured revolver to a pocket of the dun's saddlebags. And he asked a question that was uppermost in his mind: "After we're out of this, are you still going on to San Francisco?"

"I'll do whatever you ask me to, Jim," Stella answered. "Anything you think is best."

Frowning, he looked off at a line of distant peaks, etched in frozen rhythm against the sky. "I just hate to think of us being so far apart," he admitted. "I can see you had to leave Morgantown. On the other hand, surely we can find some place closer than California where you'll be safe—and where no one will guess who you are or bother you, for a while at least. Some place where we can still be in touch."

"And what about you, Jim?"

"I'm not ready to give up this fight!" His jaws

tightened. "I want, at any rate, to try and follow up that one final lead—to Wells McGraw's mistress. I'm going to ask you to stick with me. If nothing comes of it—" He got the words out with an effort. "—then I guess I'll have to accept the fact I'm never going to break the case against me. I'll give up the hiding and running. We'll leave Colorado—leave the country, if we have to, and find a place where we can start a new life. That's a promise, Stella."

She looked into his face, and her own expression reflected the troubled resolution she saw there. She leaned to place a hand on his. "It's entirely up to you," she said quietly. "I know you'll do what's best . . ."

They rode on, still climbing. Sometimes there was a glimpse of a cabin roof, or of a patch of cultivated land that marked one of the Cagle places. Bannister was painfully aware that he and Stella could themselves be highly visible at such moments, if someone in the right place on the canyon floor happened to raise his eyes and catch the hint of movement across the barren rock face. It made him anxious to get off this exposed stretch as soon as they possibly could, but it was not a trail where horses could be hurried.

It was a source of relief when they reached a point where the cliff face humped up, and the trail took them around an eroded pillar and dropped them abruptly into a shallow bowl of rock and timber. Bannister halted and turned as Stella caught up with him. "That looks to have been the worst of it," he said.

"I hope so." She was still pale, showing traces of her ordeal at the hands of her captors.

The trail twisted north again and Bannister knew they were paralleling the course of the gulch, out of sight far below. There were dim stretches over slick rock, others where the track led plainly into swales and tight stands of timber. The trees here, close to timber line, became scarcer and stunted. Overhead, clouds seemed to be gathering and they rode through their shadow into a wind that had the feel and smell of chill moisture. The shouldering peaks seemed to change shape and color, to retreat and draw nearer, with the shifting light and shadow. Bannister shook his head. A new storm might help to erase their sign, but it could add to their problems.

Then, quite without warning, a turn of the trail brought them through a screen of trees, and into a cove whose rock walls rose above them on three sides. And, at what they saw before them, they both pulled rein and Jim Bannister gave vent to a low whistle of surprise.

It was all here: the adit, its dark opening framed with pine timbers; the slag heap of broken rock; an arrastra, fashioned crudely from a pair of heavy boulders chained to a pole sweep, with a circular track created by the hoofs of the horses that walked their monotonous circle, hour after hour, working the drag that crushed the ore. Now there was no movement, no sound except the faint wind that stirred the tree heads; but from the scatter of tools—singlejacks and shovels and wheelbarrows—and even the freshness of horse droppings, it was plainly an ongoing operation. Bannister had a feeling he was beginning to get the answers to a good many questions.

Stella, at his elbow, said, "Do I see what I think I do?"

"You see it, all right," he answered. "Somebody's working ore . . ." He sent the roan forward, and dismounted to stoop for a fragment of rock that he examined carefully, and then handed up to the woman. "Have a look," he said. "I'm no miner, but I've been around Colorado long enough to know wire gold when I see it."

"It looks rich!" she exclaimed, turning the bit of ore in her fingers.

"Plenty rich! Real high grade. See there?" He indicated an open-faced pole shed, built against the rock. Beneath its slanted roof, canvas bags were neatly piled, each one crammed and bulging. "Those bags are waiting to be hauled out to a refinery. If the rock is so rotten with coarse metal that they can get stuff this rich, after putting it through a simple arrastra, then there must be a fortune stacked up in there. Someone's really made a strike!"

"The Cagles?" Stella looked at him in puzzlement. "But then, why are they still living down in that gulch, in the sheerest kind of poverty?"

"It obviously couldn't be anyone else." He added, on a different tone, "Something else is obvious, I'm afraid—about this trail we've been following."

She caught his meaning; he saw its sobering impact strike her. "Yes," she said slowly. "We know now, don't we? We thought it led outside—but instead it only leads here to the mine. It's no wonder Linda Fay didn't want to tell me anything about it!"

"We took a blind alley," Bannister agreed. He drew a long breath. "And something tells me we'd better not stay where we are . . ."

Suddenly he was anxious to be gone. Returning to his horse, he gathered the reins and had laid hold of cantle and pommel, ready to mount, when his ear caught the brittle snapping of a dry branch. He lifted his head, searching. At first he saw nothing; then in the shadow of a big pine tree, he made out the shape of a man who stood unmoving with a rifle pointed at his chest.

"That's smart, mister." The voice sounded familiar. "Don't try nothin'. You and the woman are covered, from three directions!"

Bannister lowered his boot to the ground,

and the rifleman came out of the timber with his weapon at the ready. By this time Bannister thought he had placed the voice; and the man's face, with its drooping, grizzled mustache confirmed his guess—he had seen that face before, by matchlight. And when he turned his head and saw the other pair moving up from positions where they had been waiting to help spring this trap, he was not surprised to recognize the one named Yance.

It was the latter who exclaimed, excitedly, "You see, Pa! Hit's them! Hit's the same pair give us that cock-and-bull yarn, last night—'bout runnin' away from the woman's husband! And you was the one said let 'em go."

His father nodded impatiently. "I see, all right. You fooled us good, mister," he told Bannister, and there was bitterness in his voice. "You really had us believin' you was lost pilgrims. What lies have you got now, to trot out for us?"

Bannister touched his tongue to lips that had gone dry. No kind of story would have helped, and he didn't bother. He stood with arms raised, offering no resistance as Yance came in behind him and on orders from his father made a quick search for weapons. The gun in his holster was instantly seized and passed to the older man, who merely glanced at it before shoving it behind his belt. Finding nothing else, Yance said, "He's clean, Pa."

Bannister had been holding his breath, hoping they wouldn't think to check the saddlebags on the dun and find the revolver he'd taken off Wes Dodd. But they seemed to take no interest in the horses, and they evidently thought of Stella as a woman and no kind of a threat. Bannister glanced at her and met her look of mute despair. He knew what she must be feeling—to have gone through so much, and now this!

"All right," the older man told him. "You can put 'em down."

He lowered his arms and stood waiting. There was menace in the pale eyes above that leveled rifle. Their owner was taller than most of his kin, and heavy shouldered, but for all his size he had to tilt his head in order to confront Jim Bannister; he squinted at the thin sunlight, half drowned in high mist, that fell across his face. His mouth was a hard trap between the horns of that drooping mustache.

He said crisply, "Whoever you air, I want the truth now—and I want it quick. How did you learn about this hyere dig? Who told you?"

"Nobody," Bannister replied. "We knew nothing of it at all."

He was rewarded for his answer by a stabbing slash of the rifle-barrel, directed at his face. He was able to move his head away, but even so the front sight raked a cheek, bringing the hot sting of blood. He heard Stella's quick cry; the man in front of him said through tight lips, "Quit lyin'!"

"I'm trying to tell you the truth, if you'll let me!" he retorted, angry, and aware of a warm trickle of blood upon his cheek. "You guessed one thing right, last evening—we did have someone following us, and good reason not to let ourselves be turned back." He didn't elaborate—it was plain to see these men hadn't heard yet from Vern or Dewey, or they'd have been aware of the supposed Pinkerton agent, and of the manhunt going on right now in the gulch. "We were hunting some other way out of here," he continued briefly, "and we saw this trail and took a chance. We had no idea where it went."

The pale eyes studied him suspiciously, probing. It was the young fellow, Yance, who said suddenly, "Hey Pa! Look! Last night they hadn't but one horse betwixt 'em. So, where'd they get the roan—stole it out of somebody's corral, reckon?"

That was a new thought for the older man; he scowled over it. "I'd say I knowed ever critter in the gulch—and I don't recollect this one." But he shrugged heavy shoulders. "What the hell, though! Any story he's apt to give us, stands to reason it'd only be another lie!"

"Well, whut we gonna do with 'em, now that we caught 'em, Pa?" Yance seemed to be growing restive.

"Hit's somethin' for the whole family to

decide," his father answered, "since it concerns us all. I reckon whut we'll do is take 'em down to the cabin, and call everybody together and have it out. Jeb, you fetch up the horses. Be quick!"

Jeb, a quiet fellow who might have been Yance's younger brother, turned without having said a word and hurried off into the trees. There was a time of waiting, broken by the restless movement of the dun as it shifted its weight, harness leather creaking. In the pines, a cone let loose from a high limb rustled down through lower branches, plummeted its way to earth. Bannister touched a sleeve to his cheek, which had stopped bleeding. He looked again at Stella, trying to give her reassurance but not sure he succeeded.

He turned back to the man with the rifle. "Would you be Martin Cagle? Your brother Phineas said something about you."

"Phin!" The grizzled mustache lifted in a contemptuous sneer. "So you ran into that old fool, did you? *He'd* probably take any kind of yarn you was to hand him." Suddenly the pale eyes went cold. "Was it him that told you—?"

"About this place?" Bannister shook his head firmly. "No! Not him, nor anyone. I keep saying that!"

"Yeah, I know you keep sayin' it!" Martin agreed, with high suspicion. "But at that, I imagine hit's one thing even Phin would have sense enough to keep shut about—though talk's about all he *is* good for, anymore. Was a time he used to head this family, but nowadays nobody in it gives much of a damn what he wants, or thinks!"

Jim Bannister nodded and answered drily, "That's what he indicated."

"Well, and why should they?" Martin Cagle snapped. "Who was it come here twenty years ago and found color, and persuaded the rest to get the hell out of the Ozarks and leave Missouri and the War behind them? And when that first color played out, who was it went right on huntin'—knowin' damn well those nuggets we tooken out of the creek had to of washed down from *some* place. It took till just a year ago, but I never once give up the search because it was the one way the Cagles was ever gonna advance themselves.

"Turned out I was right. I struck it rich for all of us! So, is it any wonder they follow me now, 'stead of that old fool?"

"This is a family enterprise, then?" Bannister indicated the mine, with its evidence of much continuous labor. "What do you Cagles do— work it in shifts?"

The other nodded. "With every man to share according, when time finally comes we're ready to tote our ore to the mill and collect our earnings. Until that day," he added, his pale eyes hard, "we've all tooken oath—whatever happens, nobody from outside is ever to learn about the strike. Weuns have had trouble enough keepin' claim-jumpers and such-like out of the gulch, all these years. We don't mean for word of *this* to get out!"

We all taken the oath, old Phin Cagle had remarked cryptically. Bannister had wondered then what he meant; now he understood. He understood, too, the Cagle clan's air of hostility toward all strangers. It was more than a hill people's natural seclusiveness—they were sitting on top of a secret that was more than any of them quite knew how to handle.

Now Jeb was back, mounted and leading two saddled horses by their reins. Martin Cagle swung astride a rawboned gray with a tail that looked as though the rats had been at it. He looked at Bannister, and, with a gesture of the rifle barrel, ordered him to mount.

"You'll ride in front," he said bluntly. "And you won't do nothin' careless, because this hyere rifle is gonna be pointed square betwixt your shoulder blades . . ."

Bannister merely looked at him. Yance seemed disgruntled; he said in a sour tone, "A waste of time, Pa. So we'll ride down, and we'll call the clan together and we'll talk for hours, likely. But there's only one thing we can end up doin', and you know it."

The stare that met his own was without expression. "That might be," his father told him. "But hit's for the family to vote.

"Now quit your jawin'and let's git on with this. . . ."

CHAPTER XV

A sound of someone striking metal on metal, in uneven rhythm, began to reach them as they worked their way through the trees below the rim. It lifted above the voice of the creek; then Martin Cagle, and his sons and his prisoners, broke into the open where the cabin stood, and the source of the sound revealed itself.

Wes Dodd was no longer shackled to the cabin wall where Bannister had left him. The crowbar that had freed him stood leaning against the logs, and now Dodd was on his knees before a flat slab of granite rock; he was steadying a cold chisel against a link of the handcuffs that still fastened him, by his left wrist, to the ring that had been prized loose from the wood. Vern Cagle, using a heavy maul two-handed, slammed the chisel's head repeatedly while Linda Fay and Dewey Cagle looked on, the latter with his right arm and shoulder swathed in a bulky bandage. Vern's horse stood nearby on trailing reins.

It was no surprise to Bannister that Vern seemed to be having poor luck with that tempered steel. At every stroke the chisel slipped off, chattering on rock and raising sparks; Dodd would set the bit again and Vern—evidently in a foul mood, sweating over his futile labor—raised the metal hammer for another try, to no greater success.

Aware of approaching riders, all four looked up; Vern lowered his hammer and Wes Dodd came quickly to his feet, the shackles dangling from his left wrist. It was easy to read the wary question in his glance as it passed over Bannister and Stella, and the trio who accompanied them. He could hardly fail to notice the empty holster, or guess from this that they were prisoners.

Martin Cagle scowled thunderously at sight of still another stranger. He pulled rein and demanded, "Now, who the hell is *this?* Will somebody tell me what he's doing here?"

"Pa . . ." It was Dewey who spoke up, indicating that Martin had at least one other son besides Yance and Jeb. Plainly, Dewey was hurting—his face looked nearly as white as the flour sack his wife had used to bind up the wounded shoulder. "Pa," he said, starting over, "this hyere is Mr. Dodd. He works for the Pinkertons. Me and Cousin Vern—"

"Pinkerton man, huh?" Martin looked at the stranger with new interest. Jim Bannister had already remarked the grudging respect all these people seemed to hold toward an agency detective.

Wes Dodd said in confirmation, "That's right, Mr. Cagle. And I see you've spared me some trouble. You've caught the very man I came here looking for."

"This feller, you mean?" Martin Cagle looked at Bannister, who was returning Dodd's stare with chill defiance. "You know who he is? Weuns ain't got a hell of a lot out of him, for a fact."

"He's a train robber," Vern Cagle put in. "Dewey and me are to get fifty bucks apiece, for helpin' to round him up."

And so they were still holding to that story, though Stella had learned that Vern and Dewey, both, knew perfectly well who Jim Bannister was, and the size of the bounty on him. Clearly they didn't mind lying to the rest of the family, if they could keep from splitting their share of that twelve thousand dollars.

Real family affection, Bannister thought dryly.

"Who's the woman?" Martin Cagle asked. "Is *she* wanted for anything?"

"Only for traveling with an outlaw," Dodd told him with a shrug. "But the man's a different proposition. Be sure you don't take any chances. You can see what he did to me—and with my own handcuffs!"

"Drilled me through the shoulder, Pa," Dewey added. "Wonder he didn't kill me! He's dangerous, all right—and tricky. But, me and Vern and Mr. Dodd, we'll take him off'n your hands and see he's delivered."

"Sure," Vern said quickly. "In fact, we might as well get started right now, for Ute Springs station."

They tried to make it sound as though the whole thing were settled, but Martin Cagle was not one to be hurried. Having heard them through, he scowled and leather popped and strained as he shifted in the saddle. "Just don't git ahead of yourselves," he said gruffly. "Hain't all that simple. One or two things got to be decided."

He turned to the manhunter, then, and though his manner was still respectful there was a firmness about it, that showed he wasn't to be argued with. "Sorry, Mr. Dodd. I know you got a job to do, but I'm afraid it'll have to wait this time. Yance—Jeb." He indicated the prisoners. "Bring them two inside."

"Pa!"

Martin Cagle, ignoring Dewey's wail of protest, had already dismounted; now Yance and Jeb came down from their saddles, and Bannister and Stella had no choice but to do likewise. There was little use resisting, against so many. In another moment they were being herded, none too gently, toward the cabin's open doorway.

An alarmed look passed between Dodd and Vern Cagle; the latter stepped forward as though he meant to interfere, but his uncle simply brushed past him and the younger man didn't seem quite ready to challenge authority. The prisoners were marched inside, Stella managing as best she could with her swollen ankle, and made to sit together on the edge of one of the bunks. Ropes were found, and to orders from Martin their hands were tied behind them and lashed to the bunk's timbers. Martin checked the knots. Afterward, satisfied, he turned his attention to his sons—Jeb, and Yance, and Dewey.

Apparently they all four called this shack home, with Dewey's wife to do the cooking and the chores for the lot of them. Bannister saw the way they all but filled the room; despite his own predicament, he couldn't help feeling a twinge of pity for Linda Fay who stood mute and ignored in the background, her stare pinned to her father-in-law's hard face.

"All right," Martin Cagle announced crisply. "Hit's up to you boys, now. Mount up and spread the word through the gulch—tell 'em the family has got itself a problem and that I want everybody here within the hour."

Yance said, "Everybody, Pa?"

"Every grown male." Then he corrected himself. "Well—no need to bother your uncle Phin. The old fool will talk and talk, and we'll end up gittin' no place. But, fetch everybody else." He flapped a hand at them in dismissal. "Git ridin'."

Without further questions they turned and tramped out of the cabin. Only Dewey held back; his father gave him a withering look. "Well? Whut's with *you?*"

"Pa, I ain't goin'!"

Two strides brought Martin to him, and a swing

of Martin's open palm took Dewey along the side of the skull, staggering him. "Don't tell *me* whut you ain't gonna do!" the older man roared. "You never seen the day I couldn't whup your britches. Now, go along with your brothers."

Dewey's face had drained of color; the mark of his father's palm stood out lividly. Linda Fay had given a smothered cry, and somehow she found the temerity to exclaim, "His wound's hurtin'. He cain't ride."

"Seems I remember him figurin' to ride clear down to Ute Springs Station," her father-in-law reminded her. "Boy, you go do as you're ordered. I ain't tellin' you again!"

Dewey gave up. He groaned in sheer frustration and turned away, ramming his bandaged shoulder against the side of the doorframe as he stumbled through. Outside, hoofbeats sounded as Jeb and Yance rode away on their errand; moments later, those within the cabin could hear Dewey spurring after them.

Martin Cagle had already dismissed the quarrel with his son. He went to the fireplace, evidently with intent to help himself to the contents of the big iron coffeepot on the hook; but the fire was low and he put a severe look on his daughter-in-law. "Girl, you best stir your stumps and rustle some more wood in here."

"Yes, Pa," she said meekly, and started for the door just as Vern Cagle came striding in. Vern paused there, looking at his uncle and then at the prisoners tied to the frame of the bunk, and Linda Fay slipped unobtrusively past him.

Martin, with thick-muscled arms akimbo, demanded of his nephew, "All right. Whut do *you* want?"

"Some straight answers!" Vern told him loudly—he seemed to have worked his courage up for this. "Just whut you intend doin'?"

"I've told you. Hit's for the family to say."

"You keep talkin' family—but I know damn well you've already made up your mind!"

Martin Cagle's cheeks darkened slightly; the pale eyes narrowed. "Whatever I do," he said quietly, "hit's for the good of all of us—to protect our dig, and keep the news from leakin'. And can *you* tell me more'n one way I'm to do that?"

A chill finger seemed to trace Jim Bannister's spine, having to sit here—bound and helpless—and hear the words that clearly added up to a death sentence for himself and for Stella Harbord. He shot a look at her, seeing only her profile as she watched the Cagles. He wondered if she understood, too, just what they were talking about.

Vern still wanted to argue. He said stubbornly, "Me, and Dewey, and Mr. Dodd—weuns got first claim. Don't it count, that we been runnin' our tails off tryin' to catch up with this pair?"

"For fifty dollars?" his uncle retorted. "Peanuts!"

Vern opened his mouth and then shut it again. Bannister could see in his eyes the impulse to blurt the truth about the twelve-thousand-dollar bounty. But simple greed must have won out, for Vern swallowed back his secret. Instead, he turned sullen. "Makes no difference," he insisted. "Me and Dewey earned our pay. We got a right to collect."

The older man swung his head from side to side, with an expression of deep disgust. "I tell you, I just got no patience with you—or that worthless Dewey, either! You talk about earning! Ifn you wasn't too hound-dog lazy to work your fair shift up at the mine, like all the rest of us—"

"Sure!" Vern's voice went up a notch. "You-all are really gettin' rich, ain't you? Nobody's seen a dime yet! All these months you've sweat to take a fortune in raw gold out of that damned hole— and there it lies, while we keep right on livin' here like pigs, same as ever! Well, some of us has had a damn plenty!"

So rebellion was in the open, now, and for a moment the defiant speech hung on the stillness. The room seemed to hold its breath. Outside, there was the sound of an ax chopping wood— that would be Linda Fay, busy at the chore her father-in-law had set her.

Martin Cagle had to settle his breathing before he could answer his nephew. "You've had this all explained to you. So far, our strike is the family's secret and we're all agreed we want it kept that way. Soon's the word is out—soon's we start hauling ore to the mill—you'll see these hyere mountains just a-swarmin' with claim-jumpers. They'll be all hell break loose, then; life in the gulch won't never be the same. Happens most of us Cagles ain't ready for that just yet."

Vern glared blackly at his uncle. He clenched his fists and opened them again. "All right!" he answered, and he was fairly shouting. "Go ahead—do anything you damn please! But weuns still want our prisoner. You know you got to kill him anyhow, to shut his mouth about whut he seen up there today; but then turn him over to us. Hit won't matter to Mr. Dodd. The reward pays just the same, dead or on the hoof."

"Hit do? And whut about the woman? Because, we have to shut her up, too."

Jim Bannister could hold back no longer. "Yes—what about her?" he demanded. "Twice, today, I've been told that you Cagles are law-abiding people; I think for awhile I almost believed it! But *she's* no outlaw—there's no reward out on her. Kill her and it will be plain murder! And after that, what about your so-called Pinkerton man? Will he be next?"

Fury sent Vern a step toward him, a fist cocked as though pure rage would drive it into the prisoner's unprotected face. "Mister, just shut your mouth! You're kind of late, startin' to worry about the woman. She took her chances when she hitched up with you. Wa'n't *our* fault!"

Bannister braced himself for the blow. He saw little hope for himself; it was his concern for Stella that clenched like a fist inside him and turned him reckless with the need to say something that might, in some way, save her.

But before he could answer, Martin spoke sharply to his nephew and Vern shrugged and let the fist drop, scowling. Linda Fay had just entered with a great load of chopped wood stacked in her thin, frail arms. No one offered to help with the burden. She carried it to the hearth and deposited it with a clatter, and then set to work building up the fire that had been allowed to die down.

Martin Cagle was staring hard at Bannister. He ran a raw-knuckled paw of a hand across the stubble of beard on his bony jaw. "D'you know," he grunted, suddenly, "what he says adds up, maybe. The woman surely makes a difference. Whut *do* we tell that Dodd feller? He knows she was alive when we brung her in, just now."

"Don't need to tell him nothin'," Vern answered. "He's smart enough, he won't have to ask. He don't give a damn about the woman— that's the truth. I heard him say so. Told us weuns could do with her whatever we wanted."

But Martin wasn't that easily convinced. "I dunno," he said slowly. "I dunno . . ." Suddenly his head lifted with a jerk, and he looked about as though a sudden thought had struck him. "Hey, wait a minute! Where *is* he?"

"Dodd?" Vern blinked at his uncle. "Why—outside, somewheres."

"Air you sure?"

Linda Fay looked up, then, from what she was doing at the fireplace. "If you're talkin' about that Pinkerton feller," she said, "he's done left."

They stared. Vern echoed her, a strangled exclamation: *"Left?"*

"I seen him headin' for the creek, awhile ago. On that dun horse."

"And you never told us?" her father-in-law exclaimed fiercely.

She recoiled from his look. "But—I figured you knowed . . ."

A stride that shook the cabin walls carried Martin Cagle to the doorway. He flung a look outside, then turned on his nephew; the younger man began to stammer. "Honest! I plumb forgot all about him. I told him I'd try and talk you into letting us have our prisoner. I figured he was waitin' to see how I made out."

"You did, did you? Want to know that I figure?" Martin roared back at him. "All this time, he's been outside there listenin'—which means, he heard talk about how we just might have to kill him! Now, you tell me this, boy: Has the Pinkerton man got a gun?"

Vern knitted up his brows, in painful recollection. "Not that I knowed of, Uncle Martin. *He* took it from him"—indicating Bannister—"when he strung him up with his own handcuffs, and thrun the key away. Don't see how he'd of got another."

"Then I don't blame the sonofabitch for runnin'—but we sure as hell ain't lettin' him go!" Martin Cagle rounded on Linda Fay. "You!" he told her, nodding at the prisoners lashed to the bunk frame. "You're to watch these two, hear?" Not waiting for an answer, he swung back to the door and saw Vern gaping at him. "Damn you, move!" He gave the younger man an open-palmed cuff on one shoulder, that sent him staggering through the opening.

And they were gone.

Even before the sound of their horses broke the stillness, heading for the creek, Bannister was working in a quiet fury at the rope that held him. His wrists, already raw enough from the manacles, were slippery now with sweat and blood—during the talk between Martin Cagle and his nephew he had been trying unobtrusively to do something with the knots, behind his back, though without making any headway. He went at them now with renewed vigor, setting his jaw against the pain of raw flesh—only to break off as he glanced at Stella, seated on the bunk beside him. She had slumped against the wooden frame; her head was back, her eyes closed, her breathing shallow between lips that had lost their color. Bannister spoke her name. Then Linda Fay was there, bending anxiously over her. "Somethin' wrong with your lady, mister?" the girl exclaimed.

"I think she's fainted!" he said harshly. "It wouldn't be surprising, after everything she's gone through—and then to sit and listen to them talk about killing her, and know they were dead serious about it!"

"Oh, no, mister!" Linda Fay cried. "That wa'n't but talk. They wouldn't do no such thing!" But her protest lacked conviction, and her look couldn't quite meet his. She turned again to Stella, touching a hand to her cheek.

Bannister said, "Can't you do something?"

She left them and came back with a cloth she had wrung out in cold water; wearing a look of worried concentration, she bathed Stella's face. The latter's breathing quickened. Her head jerked and her eyelids fluttered, and then she was looking around with a touch of panic, until her eyes found Bannister. "Jim?" she whispered.

As though forgetting the rope that bound her, she made a feeble attempt to rise and was forced to drop back helplessly. Linda Fay had returned, then, bearing a cup of coffee from the pot steaming above the fire. "Try some of this," she said. When Stella had got some of the strong liquid down, the girl stepped back, gnawing at her lower lip. Suddenly she turned to Bannister as she blurted, "Mister, you honest think they'd do somethin' bad to her?"

Bannister shrugged. "You know them better than I do. We found the gold mine. Will they ever believe, now, that all we're interested in is getting out of this country with our lives? Or will they kill us, to shut us up? You tell us!"

He saw her face change, saw the miserable acknowledgement of the truth. "I—" she began and broke off as her voice failed her. Her shoulders fell and she turned slowly away. Watching her, Jim Bannister forgot his own predicament enough to feel genuinely sorry for her. Remembering Marthy, he thought it must be hard to be one of the Cagle's women.

Stella was speaking. "Jim, I'm so ashamed of myself . . ."

"Don't be," he told her. "You've just taken too much."

She looked around the silent cabin. "Those men: Where have they gone?"

"Wes Dodd rode off while they were arguing— to keep from getting murdered, I imagine; and they've taken after him. He took the dun," Bannister added. "If he finds his sixshooter, that I put in the saddlebags, Vern and his uncle might be in for a surprise when they catch up with him—they think he's unarmed.

"Still, the odds are all against him. They'll deal with him, and then they'll be back. The whole clan will soon be gathering."

"And after that," she suggested, her voice breaking, "it will be our turn?"

"No!"

Linda Fay stood braced against the table, her white-knuckled hands gripping the edge of it. She was trembling and her pale cheeks shone with tears, but there was a sudden fierce resolution in her. "Lady," she cried, "hain't nobody gonna hurt you, *or* your man. I won't let 'em!" She turned suddenly, snatched something from the table, and hurried toward the bunk. It was only as she knelt at Stella's side that Bannister saw the shine of the knife blade.

"Don't do that!" he exclaimed quickly as he guessed what was in her mind. "If you want to help us, Linda Fay, you mustn't *cut* us loose— they'll know you did, and you'll be punished. Untie the rope."

She nodded and, dropping the knife, fell to work on the knots that held Stella fast to the bunk's frame. They seemed more than her clumsy, nervous fingers could deal with; growing exasperated, Bannister went back to struggling with renewed effort at his own bonds. This time, he was rewarded by feeling something slip; he was about to call out for Linda Fay to try her luck with what he had started, when he suddenly saw the ropes fall away from Stella's arms. Minutes later, both were free.

Stella took the girl into her arms and kissed her. "I only wish I knew how to thank you. . . ."

"No need for thanks, lady. I'm just hopin' to see you safe gone from here, before somebody comes back and catches you." Linda Fay turned to Bannister. "That road that leads to the mine—hit was an ol' Ute Injun trail once. I've heard Dewey say it's dim and awful hard to foller, but if you find it, it'll take you past the mine and on into the hills—the only way out, this end of the gulch."

He stared. "I'll be damned! So we guessed right, after all!" There was a last distasteful chore that had to be done. Taking the girl by the shoulders, he told her earnestly, "And now, remember this: When the men come back, you know nothing at all. You have no idea how or when I got my hands free. You watched us carefully, every minute, just as you were told—you hardly turned your back for a minute. Have you got that?"

Linda Fay nodded slowly. "I reckon . . ."

"Good girl." He drew a breath. "Sorry, Linda Fay," he muttered then, and he struck her in the jaw with his fist and caught her as she crumpled.

There was a shocked cry from Stella Harbord; as he gently placed the limp form on the bunk, he explained, "I hated like fury to do that. I'm just hoping the bruise she's going to have will keep those men from guessing she had any hand in letting us escape. Otherwise, I can't vouch for what they might do."

Stella nodded her understanding.

Bannister picked up his hat, and the sixgun Martin Cagle had taken from him and laid on the cluttered table. He said, "Now, let's get out of here!"

CHAPTER XVI

He made a face when he saw the only horse available to them—the hammerheaded roan, left standing under saddle with its reins tied to a tree beside the cabin. Bannister had developed a keen dislike for the animal. It possessed a mean streak and a mouth like leather, and he wasn't surprised that Wes Dodd, given a choice, should have helped himself instead to the dun. He wasn't even sure the roan would be persuaded to carry double, but there was nothing else for it. He jerked the reins free and was about to set toe to stirrup when he felt Stella's clutch upon his arm; he glanced at her, and followed the direction of her stare.

Over the racket of the creek, Bannister had caught no sound of a rider. He came charging straight across, his horse shouldering the current and sending up sheets of spray that obscured the shape of the man on its back. But now they reached the nearer bank, the mount scrambling for footing, and as they emerged from the willow screen Bannister saw the rider's face; it was Vern Cagle—hatless, the unshorn yellow hair whipping about his head, his mouth open on a shout. He had spotted Bannister, and there was a sixshooter in his fist.

There was no way to avoid a showdown. Jim Bannister understood: Vern had come to collect his prisoner. Twelve thousand dollars in a lump looked better than any share he might hope to get someday in the wealth of the mine; it outweighed his fear of his uncle and all the rest of the clan put together. And so he'd given Martin the slip, letting him hunt for Wes Dodd alone; and here he was.

Thinking of Stella, Jim Bannister was already running forward at an angle that would put her out of the line of fire. Now he turned and faced his enemy, bearing straight toward him.

Vern Cagle fired, point blank, at a distance of a dozen feet. Bannister felt a blow and a leg went out from under him, dropping him to one knee. He managed to catch himself; he still had his gun and with the smear of muzzle flame in his vision took blind aim, felt the revolver buck against his palm. The man in the saddle reeled and toppled. His left boot hung in the stirrup; he struck the ground on head and shoulders and then he was being dragged, bouncing limply to every reaching stride of the horse.

Bannister lurched to his feet, finding his leg already going stiff under him, and reached for the bridle as the animal pounded past. The drag of Vern's body had made it lose stride, just enough that he managed to get his fingers around leather and harness metal; he set his heels and brought the frightened horse to a mud-gouting halt. He spoke to settle it, and then looked to see what had happened to his right leg.

Vern's bullet had sliced along the outer muscle, half way between knee and hip; at the moment he felt no pain at all, but he knew it would start hurting shortly. It was a shallow wound that didn't look too serious. With Vern Cagle, however, it was a different story.

The man lay on his back, eyes closed and jaw slack, and with blood on his chest where the bullet had taken him. Bannister got his boot unhooked from the stirrup and straightened him out. In the stillness following the exchange of gunfire, Stella called anxiously.

Looking at her, Bannister shook his head. "I'm all right," he said heavily. "But Vern Cagle's dead."

There was nothing to be done for him. Bannister left him lying where he had fallen, and walked over to Stella leading the dead man's horse—a tough, if bony-looking brown. She saw the blood on the leg of his jeans and her eyes widened. "It's not bad," he said. He got out his handkerchief, to stuff into the bullet crease and soak up the bleeding. "Not enough to slow us down."

He spoke gruffly; Stella, looking at his face, read what was really troubling him. "Jim," she said earnestly, "Vern Cagle would have killed *you*. You had to defend yourself."

"He was after the reward," Bannister said in a dead voice. "Under the law, I'm fair game. But if *I* happen to kill someone—even to save my own life—it only adds to the score against me . . ." This was a bitter truth he had learned to live with, and he shrugged it away.

Cagle's bronc seemed a tractable animal— *Horse stealing again,* he thought grimly; still, they really needed the brown if they had any hope of getting out of this place. He helped Stella into the saddle, and mounted the roan, the hurt leg stretching and causing him to wince. But it had stopped bleeding already, and, satisfied that it was not a serious hurt he closed his mind to the pain.

The long and wearing day was drawing to its close. In another hour the sun would be dropping toward the peaks, veiled now in thickening drifts of mist that had settled as the afternoon wore on; and they had to find that Ute trail they'd been told of, before night overtook them.

There was no time to waste.

Being acquainted now with the route as far as the Cagles' gold strike, Bannister was able to set a good pace. As they climbed, it was almost as though the clouds came down to meet them. Color gradually left the world as the sun's rays were blotted up; then streaks of mist were sifting through the upper branches of stunted pines,

225

wheeling overhead. Their breath and that of the horses rose in gray plumes. The day had turned dankly chilly—Stella, huddled in Bannister's coat, seemed to be doing well enough, and when she asked anxiously about his leg, he smiled and shook his head. "Don't worry about it."

Just now he was concerned less about his physical discomfort than how they would fare even if they managed to locate the old trail, with early night soon to fall. But he said nothing of that to Stella.

When they reached the cove and the mine, they found that some freakish trick of air currents had collected the mist so that it drifted in layers here, like a heavy fog, through which the surrounding timber and rock faces rose eerily; the entrance of the dig was a blackly gaping mouth in a face without features. Dusk already lay close at hand, Bannister debated just how to start looking for an Indian trace that was certain to be dim at best. Trees ghosted by; the horses' hoofs were muffled in the carpet of ancient needles as they moved through a world without shape or sound.

Then Bannister did hear something, and he quickly pulled rein and motioned Stella to a halt. The sound was repeated—faint but definite, as of someone working with loose rock. He frowned, trying to make it out. It had not occurred to him that any of the Cagles would have been left behind, when Martin and his sons left to call a meeting of the entire clan. Stella started to voice a question. He silenced her and gave her his reins to hold as he eased out of the saddle, drawing his gun.

Tension high in him, Bannister paced forward, favoring the hurt leg as he set his boots carefully and at each step probed the fog for a glimpse of this potential enemy. Whoever it was seemed unaware of him, wholly absorbed with his task. By now the sounds were very close . . . Suddenly, the curtains of mist shook and parted on an eddy of chill air, and Bannister saw his man.

With a saddled horse waiting nearby, he was putting the capstone to a small rock cairn he had just finished constructing. The horse was Jim Bannister's dun. The man was Wes Dodd.

His head turned and they both stared, frozen in complete surprise. Bannister was first to find his voice. "You're supposed to be running—to save your hide from the Cagles!"

The manhunter made no answer. He stood half bent, narrow face unreadable, eyes on the gun the other held. And Jim Bannister suggested, "You must really have got an earful, listening outside that cabin. What did you want, to see for yourself just what was up here?"

Now Wes Dodd straightened, slowly; the handcuffs, still dangling from his left wrist, clinked faintly. There was something about him that suggested a coiled spring. "Don't tell me," he

227

said harshly, "that you're not thinking along the same line."

"Am I?"

"Isn't it obvious? Thanks to those dumb Cagles, here's a gold mine and a fortune, just waiting for any man who stakes and registers his claim to it. To you it means wealth enough to give even the syndicate a battle—buy off the right officials, and get that murder charge quashed. You're saying you never thought of that?"

Actually, he hadn't—the notion of trying to rob the Cagles of their gold had never entered his head. But Wes Dodd would undoubtedly judge him a liar if he said so; Bannister merely returned the other's look, and Dodd misread his silence. The narrow mouth quirked.

"Just as I said—it's obvious. And to that extent at least, you and I are in the same boat, Bannister: We're both looking for the main chance. Bounty collecting is a sucker's game—it pays almost as bad as wearing a star. But here, we've got plenty for us both.

"You're an outlaw—no way in the world you could hope to register a mining claim. I'll take care of that detail, and you'll help me stand off the Cagles when they try to make it a fight, as they're bound to do. You see, there's every reason in the world for us to settle our differences, and work this out together . . ."

He trailed off. At every word he had been

talking a little faster, a little louder; and Bannister suddenly realized the man was talking for his life. With a gun pointed at his chest, he was marshaling every argument that would stay Bannister's hand on the trigger. When he got no response at all, Dodd's cool exterior seemed suddenly to crack. His chest lifted on a tremulous breath. "You wouldn't shoot a man in cold blood!"

"No?" Bannister retorted, through set lips. "They seem to think so in New Mexico. And there's twelve thousand dollars of syndicate money says I would—money you were more than anxious to collect, an hour ago!" But then he shook his head and lowered the gun, as he said resignedly, "Whatever you've heard, the fact is I've never killed any man unless my back was against the wall, and my life depended on it. Today I killed Vern Cagle. I'm in no hurry to add another to the list."

Wes Dodd didn't believe him. He peered at Bannister through the drifting wavers of fog as, nervously, he rubbed the wrist that still wore the encircling steel of his own handcuffs. He said, "So, what *are* you planning to do with me?"

"I just don't know," Bannister admitted honestly. "I suppose that's up to you, isn't it?"

Without any warning, Wes Dodd's right hand slid the few inches into the gap of his coat and came out holding a gun. There was only time to think, *so he did check the dun's saddlebags!* Then Bannister was trying to raise the weapon he'd lowered, panic touching him as he saw how swiftly the manhunter had made his move.

Wes Dodd moved *too* swiftly; the coiled spring of his nerves responded before the gun was quite on target. It exploded prematurely and the bullet just missed Bannister's elbow. Then he was firing, and the two shots blended. Powder smoke mingled with the drifting fog. He saw Wes Dodd flung about, to stagger and fall to his knees. He dropped in a sprawl on the cairn of loose stones he had constructed, toppling it.

Bannister heard Stella calling anxiously; he answered, "It's all right." Now she came leading the roan by its leathers, appearing to forget all about the injured ankle when she swung down to search his face for reassurance. Only then did she see the man he had shot.

"Why, it's Wes Dodd! Is he—?"

"Yes. He's dead." Bleakly: "As dead as Vern Cagle!"

"What was he doing *here?*"

"A little claim-jumping." Bannister eased breath into his cramped lungs. "He fooled the Cagles by laying a pretend trail for them across the creek; then he doubled back, to take a look at this dig for himself. He told me he was always one to look for the main chance . . ."

An empty tomato tin had been enclosed in

the cairn, rolling a little way as the stones were scattered; Bannister stooped and picked it up. He was just straightening with it, wincing at the pull of bullet-torn leg muscle, when he and Stella both became aware of a growing sound of horses.

They were just entering the cove. The high, encircling walls caught up the echoes of hoof-beats and multiplied them, bounced them around deceptively until they might have been a troop of cavalry pouring from a dozen directions at once. Jim Bannister's first reaction was to seek cover, but he could see no likely hiding place; and by then it was already too late to mount. The best he could do was to put Stella behind him, and set himself with his revolver ready, and wait.

Then they came bursting out of the fog, a half dozen of them—Martin Cagle, Heck, Dewey with his bandaged arm, others of the clan who were unknown to Bannister. He reasoned that they must be homing in on the exchange of gunshots; if so, the battered echoes had fooled them, too. They almost overran Bannister and the woman. Barely in time, someone shouted and then there was a hauling of reins, a startled milling of horses.

He held his ground and heard Dewey cry out: "Here he is! *Hyere's* Vern's murderer, the sonofabitch!"

It was Dewey's blackbearded cousin Heck, apparently, who first noticed the body at

Bannister's feet. "By damn!" he shouted. "Now he's gone and killed the Pinkerton man!"

The animals had been settled by this time, more or less, and with one accord the Cagles quieted as they turned to their leader. While they watched, Martin slowly rubbed a fist over his grizzled mustache, considering. He nodded finally. "Might be all for the good," he pointed out. "One less for us to get rid of."

And having said that, he threw his reins and deliberately stepped down, carrying his rifle. Young Dewey joined his father.

All of them were bristling with weapons, but Bannister stood fast with his revolver trained now on Martin's thick chest. He said sharply, "Stay back!"

"There's a half dozen of us," Martin Cagle reminded him. "And only one of you. You might's well drop that."

"No! You've seen by now that I can use it. I don't want to," Bannister insisted. "I'm telling the truth when I say I never wanted to kill Vern, if he hadn't forced me. Can you and I talk, instead?"

"What the hell is there to talk about?"

"This, for a start." Bannister tossed him the tomato tin. The man caught it with his free hand, looked at it incuriously and again at Bannister as the latter said, impatiently, "Well, look inside."

Scowling and suspicious, Martin peered into

the tin; apparently he saw something, for he hung the rifle over an arm, freeing his other hand so he could probe the interior with a couple of fingers. The paper he drew out might have been a page ripped from a notebook. He muttered something, threw the can away and, unfolding the paper, held it up to squint at it in the rapidly fading light.

Abruptly his head jerked; Bannister, seeing the look that came over him, nodded grimly. "I think you get the idea. The man was putting up boundary markers, staking a claim—on your gold mine!"

Someone said hoarsely, "The hell he was!"

"Why not?" Bannister had to raise his voice, to continue making himself heard. "It's here for the taking. All he'd have had to do was ride down to the nearest registry office, and it would have been legally his. Every bit of your work gone for nothing—and not a damn thing any of you could have done about it!

"You've shown you'd go to any length, trying to keep strangers away," he went on, into a silence that had grown weighted and dangerous. "But then one outsider was finally welcomed into the gulch—this man Dodd; and you see what he nearly did to you! The next time, you might not be so lucky."

"Next time?" Martin Cagle stirred his heavy shoulders. "There hain't gonna be no next time. We'll just have to make sure."

"By killing the two of us, I suppose! Do you really think that will stop it?" Bannister's throat felt tight and raw with the intensity of his arguing. In effect he was pleading for his own life and Stella's, but as he looked at these implacable faces he could see no sign that he was making any impression. "News as big as this strike can't be kept a secret forever. Believe me, the thing you should do—"

"We ain't askin' advice from no outlaw!" Dewey cut him off harshly.

"But hit do appear," someone broke in, "that you air gittin' some—and sounds like it could be worth hearin'!"

Nobody seemed to have noticed the arrival of newcomers. Now, heads lifted and turned and then held motionless, as Phin Cagle came out of the fog with Charlie riding close behind his grandfather. The old man was hatless; wraiths of mist clung to his wispy hair and chopped-off beard and made him more frail, more ethereal than ever. He drew up beside Martin and looked at him from the batched and battered saddle. He said, "You by God had better listen."

Martin Cagle found his voice and it came out in a roar of rage. "You damned old fool! Don't give *me* orders!"

Instantly, his milky stare showing no change of expression, Phin lashed out with a boot toe. It took the other flush on the jaw and sent him

234

staggering, to lose his footing and go down flat on his shoulders; while the tightly grouped horses snorted and moved around uneasily, Martin Cagle lay there looking stunned. He stared at the old man, who leaned over him now, one gaunt arm stabbing a bony, pointing finger down at him.

"Trouble with you," old Phin told his brother, "you're jist too big for your britches! You hear me?" He got no answer. His words dripped with scorn as he went on, regardless: "Back when we was sprouts, I used to knock sense into that thick skull of yours ever once in a while. I never should of left off, never should of let you git the idea you was smart enough to take charge of runnin' this family! Like today—puttin' out the call for a big meetin', and me not even knowin' about it till Charlie here got wind, somehow or other . . . Now, you git up from there," he added sternly. And when the other made no move: "I said, *git up!* No, leave the rifle!"

Martin had begun looking about for the weapon he'd dropped when he fell. He let it go now. Meekly enough, almost as in a daze, he picked himself off the ground and the change in him was astonishing. All the bluster and loudness were gone; he behaved like someone who had been chastised and put in his place. He stood mutely rubbing his jaw where Phin's boot toe had landed, as though he were waiting to be told what to do.

All he'd really needed, Bannister understood in

some amazement, was for his brother Phin to put his foot down, at last, and reassert an authority Martin Cagle had long ago been trained to respect. . . .

"Now then," the oldest Cagle said sternly, "the lot of you will pay attention! Go ahead, mister." He nodded to Bannister. "You finish whut you was a-sayin', just now."

Bannister took a breath—still dazed at the turn of events, but feeling he was past being, ever again, surprised at anything. "All I meant to say," he told the bunch of them, "is that you people are making a damned big mistake. Here you are, after twenty years, still living in poverty that turns your young women old, and your young men into rebels—and no wonder, when they see you sitting on a fortune, and nobody getting any good from it. You can't expect them to wait forever, any more than you can hope to keep the mine a secret forever.

"Before it's too late, you'd better do what should have been done months ago, when you first stumbled onto this gold of yours. There's enough of you, that you can nail down any claim here that looks at all promising. And once they're legally staked and registered, it will be up to the law to help protect them when the claim-jumpers come. Go on the way you are, and sooner or later you risk losing it all!" Bannister paused to look at the stolid and expressionless faces. He shook his head then as he told Phin Cagle, "They're not listening."

"Oh, they air listening," the old man assured him. "Alls they need is a little time for it to sink in. Right now," he added, "daylight's goin' fast, and this fog's beginnin' to stiff up my joints some. You and your lady fetch your hosses, so's we can be headin' back down to my cabin."

Bannister had slid his gun into the holster but he kept his hand on it. He looked at Stella, and again at the old man. "I don't know. After everything that's happened, I think we'd as soon not go back into that gulch."

"Don't see how you got a choice. There's an old Injun trail up here somewheres, but you'd never foller it in the dark. Git lost in these damn mountains and you'll freeze to death.

"Anyway," Phin added, "I don't imagine either of you's been eatin' regular, lately. You-uns need a good, hot meal, and a comfortable bed. And looks like you got a leg, there, that needs something done for it. Tomorrow's soon enough to leave—I'll guarantee, hain't nobody gonna give you any trouble." As he said it, he gave his kin a stern look that held both a message and a warning.

But Dewey could contain himself no longer. "Don't it matter," he cried, in a voice turned shrill with protest, "this hyere's the sonofabich that killed Vern?"

His uncle looked at him coldly. "I figure we all know he couldn't help that. He also saved our gold mine, so I'd say we got the best of the trade!" He indicated the body of Wes Dodd. "Git rid of that thing," he ordered. "Hardly matters much how. I don't think he was any Pinkerton man—I don't reckon anybody at all is gonna miss him." And turning to Bannister: "You two ready?"

Jim Bannister had already led up the dun, from where Wes Dodd had left it on trailing reins. In a dead silence he helped Stella to mount, and again took the roan's saddle. His hand was not far from the gun in his holster, and every nerve was taut as he kneed the horse into motion under the watchful stares of the Cagles; yet no one spoke, or tried to interfere. He and Stella rode past them, unimpeded.

Suddenly Dewey Cagle was shouting, in a last hysterical outburst: "Damn it, listen to me! That's Jim Bannister. The sonofabitch is worth twelve thousand—"

His father's growl cut him off. "Didn't you hear?" Martin Cagle muttered. "Everything's been settled. Now, shet up!"

Then Phin and his dim-witted grandson closed in behind Stella and Bannister, leaving the group beside Wes Dodd's body. Voices faded. Wraiths of mist, and settling darkness, quickly swallowed them. . . .

Center Point Large Print
600 Brooks Road / PO Box 1
Thorndike, ME 04986-0001 USA

(207) 568-3717

US & Canada:
1 800 929-9108
www.centerpointlargeprint.com